No Place Like
HOME

Also by Dee Romito

The BFF Bucket List

Best. Night. Ever.
with coauthors

No Place Like HOME

Dee Romito

Aladdin

New York London Toronto Sydney New Delhi

ALADDIN

An imprint of Simon & Schuster Children's Publishing Division

1230 Avenue of the Americas, New York, New York 10020

First Aladdin hardcover edition September 2017

Text copyright © 2017 by Dee Romito

Jacket illustration copyright © 2017 by Annabelle Metayer

Also available in an Aladdin M!X paperback edition.

All rights reserved, including the right of reproduction in whole or in part in any form.

ALADDIN and related logo are registered trademarks of Simon & Schuster, Inc.

For information about special discounts for bulk purchases, please contact Simon & Schuster Special Sales at 1-866-506-1949 or business@simonandschuster.com.

The Simon & Schuster Speakers Bureau can bring authors to your live event. For more information or to book an event contact the Simon & Schuster Speakers Bureau at 1-866-248-3049 or visit our website at www.simonspeakers.com.

Jacket designed by Jessica Handelman

Interior designed by Tom Daly

The text of this book was set in Excelsior LT Std.

Manufactured in the United States of America 0817 FFG

2 4 6 8 10 9 7 5 3 1

Library of Congress Control Number 2017932243

ISBN 978-1-4814-9109-9 (hc)

ISBN 978-1-4814-9108-2 (pbk)

ISBN 978-1-4814-9110-5 (eBook)

For Nathan and Kiley.
You are my greatest adventure.

chapter one

When I was little, I used to wish I could fly. I dreamed of soaring through the air and seeing the world from far above it—with the houses and trees becoming so tiny I could put them in a dollhouse, and all the little automobiles turning into toy cars before my eyes. But I'm pretty sure that somewhere along the line, the universe got its signals seriously crossed, because this life of mine isn't *quite* what I meant.

"Dad, can I please finish my dessert before I do the essay on the thirteen colonies?" I ask. Does it count as school when you're thirty thousand feet in the air and your dad is your teacher?

A blob of warm, fudgy icing slides down the

side of my brownie and helps make my point.

"Sure. I have something to talk to you about anyway." Dad pushes his tray into the arm of his seat (yeah, fancy contraptions in the fancy seats) and turns to face me.

Translation: serious conversation.

I dig my fork into the brownie and shove a big mound of it in my mouth.

"I know it's hard for you to be flying all over the country like this, Kenzie," says Dad. "You don't get to do a lot of the things other twelve-year-olds do."

We've had this conversation before. Dad tells me how sorry he is that his job forces us to travel all the time. No, literally, ALL THE TIME. We don't spend more than a few days in one place before we're on our way to the next stop. He's a consultant for companies trying to go green, yet we guzzle up fuel like crazy getting to all his meetings. Kind of ironic.

We lost my mom three years ago, and while Dad couldn't afford to give up his job, he also wasn't about to go anywhere without me anymore. On that first day we were on our own, those were his exact words. He knelt down in front of me, gently grabbed my hands, and said, "Kenzie, I'm not about to go anywhere without you anymore."

So he told his company he wouldn't fly international (uh, hello, Dad—Paris and London?!) and that they had to let me travel with him. That's our deal and I get it. I always tell him it's okay, and that it's actually sort of fun staying in fancy hotels and getting to see different cities, because it is.

What I don't say is that I miss having my own bed, a place for my things, and a best friend I can see every day.

"Sweetie, are you listening to me?" asks Dad.

Clearly, I haven't been. There's chocolate on my chin, and Dad's face is all excited-looking. I totally missed something.

"Sorry, what did you say again?" I ask. "Ooh, did they approve the assignment in Minnesota? Because you said next time we could go to the Judy Garland Museum." *The Wizard of Oz* is my all-time favorite movie, but we've had to skip the museum the last three times. Fun side trips aren't easy to squish into jam-packed meeting days.

Dad laughs. "No, that's not it. I said we're staying in Las Vegas for about six weeks."

It takes me a good ten seconds before I really get what he's saying. "Six *weeks*?" I ask. My mouth drops open, and not for another bite of brownie.

"What? Why? I mean, how is that even possible?"

Dad smiles like he's amused by my response. "This one's a big project. They rented us a house, and I was thinking you might want to enroll in the local middle school for—"

"Yes, please!" I don't even give him a chance to finish. "A real school with real kids and lunches full of tater tots and those cute little milk containers? Who wouldn't want that?"

Dad chuckles again. "It sounds fun, doesn't it?"

Yes, it so does. KIDS. Like, people my size, not dressed in business suits or hotel-employee uniforms. No chaperone assigned to me while my dad is in meetings. Teachers who don't go totally overboard with assignments and projects. I haven't been to an actual school in a while, but I'm pretty sure they're still the same.

Dad takes my enormous smile as a yes. "Okay, then, it's settled," he says. "We'll take care of the paperwork as soon as we get there."

Although Vegas isn't where we're headed now. We've got Chicago, Santa Fe, and Denver to hit first.

Dad glances over at my essay notes and taps his finger on the paper. "'Foreign' doesn't follow the *i*-before-*e* rule, remember?" He taps again, this time at the bottom. "And two *n*'s in 'tyranny.' But otherwise it's looking good, sweetie."

I correct the mistakes, circle them, and add a couple of stars as reminders. They will most definitely be on this week's spelling test.

"But I guess we can skip the essay for now," Dad adds casually.

Yes! Homework pass for the win.

Dad gets up to use the bathroom, and everyone else in first class is either asleep or has headphones on, so for a few minutes it's like I have the place to myself. I quietly sing the chorus of "We're Off to See the Wizard," bopping my head from side to side. And to top it all off, the flight attendant asks if I'd like another brownie. FYI, the answer to that is always yes.

After the one-day trips to Chicago and Santa Fe, we arrive in Denver, exhausted. These shorter trips totally wear me out.

Our first stop is always to see Fiona at the hotel concierge desk. They're the people who take care of whatever you need (dinner reservations, tickets to a show, a toothbrush because you forgot yours), and regulars like my dad get to know them pretty well.

"My favorite guests!" says Fiona when she sees us. Her beautiful British accent is quite possibly my favorite ever.

She comes out and gives us each a big hug, and I immediately catch the familiar scent of her lilac perfume. She's the kind of absolutely gorgeous that makes it impossible not to notice her instantly. She *seems* almost as tall as my dad, although I'm guessing she'd lose about four inches without the heels.

"I'll phone the kitchen and order a fresh apple pie," she says. We don't bother telling her we'll never finish it all, because she'll insist anyway. Fiona uses only two words when she calls the kitchen—"VIP" and "pie." "You can take what you can't finish back to your room," she says when she hangs up.

The three of us find a comfy spot in the lobby because Fiona also insists we relax when we get here. She's one of the reasons I love this place.

"How have you been?" Dad asks her.

But Fiona waves him off. "My life is nowhere near as interesting as yours. What have you been up to, Kenzie?" She loves hearing about where we've been, even if all I have to say is that I got to order an ice cream sundae from room service in New York City.

"Well, there is something exciting," I say. Her eyes open wide, and I hope I don't disappoint her. "We're staying in Las Vegas for a while, and I get to go to middle school for six weeks." I try not to jump all over the place with excitement, but Fiona does it for me. She slaps her hands on the glass table between us, and her chair scoots back a few inches.

"Six weeks? Middle school? How fabulous!" The lobby chatter quiets down for a few seconds, but people quickly go back to their conversations. "Lucky girl. You'll make lots of new friends."

"I hope so," I say. "I mean, I won't be there long enough for anything major, but it'll be nice to be around other kids."

Dad excuses himself to go get us some water. As if he needs to get it himself. All Dad has to do is tip a finger in the air and they'll bring him whatever he wants. Regular guests get *really* good service.

"But six weeks, that's half a term," says Fiona with a smile. "You'll adore it!"

Her enthusiasm is yet another thing I love about

her. Plus, she's put into words exactly what I've been thinking. I have six weeks to be a kid in middle school. Six weeks to have a normal life and actually live in one place for more than a weekend. I didn't even realize how badly I wanted that until now.

"You're totally right," I say. "As always."

Dad is heading back to us, and Joanne from the Nannies to Go agency Dad uses walks through the front door. She gives me a high five with her red, manicured nails hitting the tips of my fingers. I'm happy to see it's Joanne, because she always has some grand adventure planned for us. Although Denise (the other nanny I adore here—I call her Denver Denise) takes me to the absolute best restaurants.

"Did you finish all your homework on the plane?" asks Joanne.

I nod. "What are we doing today?" I ask.

"It's a surprise," she says. "But let's just say your nails will never have looked better, your feet will be totally smooth, and you'll be able to tell all your friends you saw the hottest new movie."

"So it's not a surprise," I joke. And as much as I can't wait for my next adventure in middle school, I have to admit I might miss all this pampering a little.

chapter two

'm a weird mix of nervous and excited like it's my first day of kindergarten. Dad insisted that he walk me into school to make sure I was all set, but I insisted even more that he absolutely not. We had already toured the school when we got here from Denver on Tuesday. I know my locker combination, and I have my schedule. I'm as ready as I'm going to be.

I step through the big glass doors to Sagebrush Middle and into a sea of kids. And, technically, while it's my first day, everyone else has already been in school for more than a month.

I should be watching where I'm going, not eyeing all the middle-schoolness around me. Instead I smack right into a girl with short dark hair propped on top of her head with an elastic headband.

I should say I'm sorry.

Help her pick up her books.

But I just stand there.

This is so not like elementary school.

"Are you okay?" she asks.

I'm still not moving. What is wrong with me?

"I'm Ashia," says the girl, apparently not fazed by my stone-statue look.

"Kenzie," I manage to squeak out.

"Well, hello, Kenzie," she says. "I'm guessing it's your first day?"

I nod.

"Don't worry—this place looks like a zoo, but it's pretty easy to get around." She draws out her vowels the tiniest bit with an exotic accent I can't place. I wonder if I still sound like a Northern Californian.

"Thank you," I say. "It's all a little much."

And just when I think I can do this, the cutest boy I've ever seen rushes past me. I don't even try to hide the head whip I do to catch another glimpse of him.

Ashia laughs. "That's Tate O'Dea. I can introduce you later if you'd like."

I shake my head. "No way. I mean, no thank you."

"Okay, but the offer stands. So, do you know where you're going?" she asks.

"Not really." Even though I was here a couple days ago with my dad, it all looks so different with the halls full of kids. I pull my schedule from my backpack and hand it over. "Can you help me find my homeroom?"

"Sure. I'll walk you there," she says. "Ooh, and we have the same lunch period! You'll have to sit with me."

On the way, she points out all the things I need to know, like where the nicest hall monitors sit; how to avoid the principal, Mr. Kumar, at all costs; and a secret shortcut to my first class. She promises to meet me at lunch, which makes me feel better already.

"And you should totally join drama club," says Ashia. Her "totally" comes out as a beautiful "toe-tuh-lee." "Tryouts for the musical are after school today."

I secretly love to sing. In the shower. Giving a concert in our hotel room. In the rental cars with Dad. But not in front of anyone else.

"I'm more the stage-crew type," I say.

Ashia nods. "Whatever you want, but you do have excellent timing. We're doing a classic this year."

I'm still stuck on the way she says "egg-cellent" when she gives me a light smack on the shoulder. "Oh, sorry, right. A classic. Which one?" I ask.

"*The Wizard of Oz*," says Ashia. "It doesn't get any better than that."

No, it sure doesn't. Not in a million years would I have expected fate to plop down in front of me like this. I stop in my tracks and grab my new friend by the shoulders.

"Did you say *The Wizard of Oz*?" I ask.

She nods.

"It's my all-time, can't-possibly-convince-me-it's-not-the-best-movie-ever, favorite," I say. But then my shoulders droop. "Never mind. I couldn't possibly stand up in front of all those people and talk, let alone sing." Plus, I'll be long gone before the performances. But I don't tell her that yet.

We walk again, in what I'm guessing is the direction of my homeroom.

"You can do anything you want to do," she says.

Yeah, if only.

"Think about it." Ashia points to the open doorway we're now standing in front of. "This is your stop. I'll see you at lunch."

And in an instant she's off down the hall. I turn to face a classroom full of new faces.

I'm a whole lot more nervous than I thought I'd be today, but at least I have tater tots and Ashia to look forward to.

I take a seat up front in English class.

To act like I'm not totally out of place, I open up one of my notebooks to write my name inside. But my chair is jolted from behind, and my pencil flies across the paper.

The boy behind me mouths a *Sorry* when I turn around.

Ten seconds later, it happens again.

This time I jump into airplane passenger mode. It doesn't happen very often in first class, but when Dad and I have to fly coach (I'm not a snob, really I'm not, but first class is all kinds of AWESOME), having a kid kick my seat is a pretty regular thing. Unfortunately.

I turn around and get my friendly face ready. On try number one, you go for polite. "Maybe you don't realize that every time you do that, my chair moves," I say to the boy behind me.

"Right. Sorry," he says out loud this time.

Students are still coming in, chatting with their friends as they make their way to their seats. The teacher is busy flipping through her plan book and doesn't seem to notice all the noise.

I go back to writing, and this time I'm trying to jot down the notes from the board when my head jolts and my chair moves forward a good two inches.

On try number two, you lay out the consequences. This requires a stern look.

"Listen, I don't appreciate having my chair kicked. I suggest you stop it or . . ." Wait, what are the consequences in a classroom? Telling the teacher and becoming the class tattletale is probably not the best move.

"Or?" asks the boy, daring me to finish my sentence.

I dive into my bag of tricks and manage to find one that might work. "Or the sticky red juice I have in my lunch bag might accidentally squirt behind me and you'll need a good soapy bath after school." Not my best (especially since I don't actually have a lunch bag), but it works especially well with active little boys on planes. As long as their parents can't hear me, that is.

"I don't bathe often," says the boy with a smirk. "So that would be a disaster." He sits up straight and plants his feet firmly on the floor.

Good. He does *not* want to see try number three.

As soon as the bell rings, Mrs. Pilchard smacks a stack of brochures on her desk. "We have one item of business to get out of the way first. The countywide poetry contest begins today, and you have one week to submit your entries. Five winners will be chosen, and if you're one of those winners, you'll get a very nice prize pack, your poem will be published in the local newspaper, and you'll have the chance to read it aloud at a fancy awards dinner. I'd consider it if I were you."

Darn. She had me until "read it aloud." No chance of that happening. And fancy dinners certainly aren't anything new to me. Still, I eye that pile of pamphlets on the way out of class, debating whether or not to grab one.

I don't.

The hall is like an airport terminal at Chicago O'Hare. Luckily, I've already mapped out my route to lunch, so I keep walking straight until I need to make a right turn. When I finally make it to what I've been told to call "the caf," I search frantically for Ashia. Shoulder bumps from the crowd keep knocking me from side to side, so I get out of the way and head for the lunch line.

Once I have my food (stuffed-crust pizza day!), I scan the room again for Ashia. Right now I'm wishing I had a solid seat assignment. Seriously, the world of airplane travel has gotten that right. It would at least make this new-kid-in-the-cafeteria thing much easier.

"Kenzie!" Ashia is running toward me like I'm her long-lost puppy. "You'll still sit with me, yes?"

I nod and follow her, grateful to have someone to have lunch with. A *friend* to have lunch with.

"Hey, everybody, this is Kenzie." She rattles off the names of the girls at the table, and when she gets to the end, she points toward the lone boy. "And this is Bren Clarke. Our resident book nerd."

He turns his attention to Ashia. "We've met. Sort of," he says. "She sits in front of me in English."

It's not until now that I notice what his T-shirt says. I READ. WHAT'S YOUR SUPERPOWER?

Maybe he's not as bad as I thought.

"I'm Bren." He sticks out his hand.

I take it and give a strong shake like my dad taught me. "Kenzie," I say. "But for now I'm going to call you Beckham, since you kick like him."

Bren laughs. "Well played, Kenzie," he says. "Well played."

Ashia nudges me. "You two done flirting? Lunch is only thirty minutes." She sits down, leaving me standing there with heat rushing to my face.

"We weren't—"

"It's a joke. Sit down." Ashia motions to the open spot.

For the next ten minutes, Ashia tries again to convince me to try out for the musical. I consider telling her exactly why I can't, but she's so excited that I let her keep talking.

"She should join book club," says Bren, popping his nose out of the book he's been reading. "We do some really cool field trips. And we have an author visit in the spring."

I don't want to admit that book club is right

up my alley. "Are you in charge of book club?" I ask Bren. But before he can answer, someone is singing across the room, and the caf goes silent as everyone turns to watch.

"What's going on?" I ask.

"Remember cute Tate from this morning?" says Ashia. "Dude can sing."

He's seriously belting out a love song to one of the girls sitting next to him, and all the awestruck girls in the lunchroom are watching like they're at a boy-band concert. Even the boys are hooting and hollering.

"Yeah, but . . ." I stop, wondering if school has turned into a real-live *High School Musical* or *Grease* while I've been in the air. "Is this . . . normal? Does it happen at other schools too?"

"Totally not," says Ashia. "But he loves the attention and we love the show, so the teachers don't mind. Music is kind of our thing here."

Not only is Cute Tate adorable, but he also has an amazing voice. It's crazy to me that he can stand up there on the table bench and sing to a "sold-out" cafeteria. I could never. But Ashia's right: I'm loving the show.

When the song is over, the crowd claps and

cheers, including the teachers and the lunch ladies.

"You know, Tate will most certainly be in the musical," Ashia whispers.

I try to hold back a smile but totally fail at it.

"Meet you at tryouts after school?" she asks.

I nod. If it means hearing that voice every day I'm here, I might need to reconsider.

chapter three

Bren is standing in the auditorium doorway when I get there after school. He hands me a pamphlet.

"I saw how you looked at those poetry-contest pamphlets," he says. "Not sure why you didn't take it yourself, but I figured you might want one."

Before I can even say thank you, and tell him I have no intention of entering, he's gone. Sucked into the mass of kids in the hallway like he's gone through a portal to another dimension.

"O-kay." I shove the pamphlet in my bag and head in to find Ashia. She's front and center with a clipboard on her lap.

"Kenzie!" She definitely wins for most enthusiastic in this place. "You're trying out, right?"

It all looks so fun and I kind of wish I could. "I'm here to see you try out. I can't do it, though."

"Sure you can. It's a great time. And after all the shows are done, we have this incredible cast party," she says. "The only not-so-good part of it all is that Shelby Jacobs will probably get the lead."

"Who's Shelby Jacobs?" I ask.

Ashia points to the left side of the stage, where a girl in a fancy dress with short red hair is getting ready for her audition. "Let's just say her amazing voice is her best quality, and I couldn't name another one."

"Yikes," I say. "I'll be sure to steer clear of her."

When Shelby glides up to the microphone and sings, I sit back in shock. She's incredible.

But Ashia doesn't seem to notice. "You're going up, right?"

The lead is obviously securely Shelby's, and it would be kind of nice to get some feedback on my singing. *If* I could actually get the words to come out of my mouth.

"I can't go up there and sing in front of everyone," I say.

The girl next to me explains that they'll call

kids up for the chorus at the same time, and all I have to do is sing with the group and say a few lines of dialogue with a partner.

Hmm. Maybe I *can* do this.

Mom always told me I had a beautiful voice, and my dad says I'm a star in the making, but parents are supposed to say that. Teachers, on the other hand, don't have to say anything nice if they don't want to. And if I somehow manage to get cast, I can quietly tell the adviser to take me off the list.

"Okay, fine. I'll try," I say. "But if I step up there and panic, you have to come save me."

"Of course," says Ashia.

More kids filter in as Ashia and I sign our names on the tryout sheet under "chorus."

As the auditions continue, my hands get shaky and I can't keep my foot still.

My group is called to the stage and asked to sing "Follow the Yellow Brick Road" as the teachers in charge walk around with clipboards, taking notes. One of the teachers gets real close and leans in like she's listening intently. I try to stay focused, but, oh man, what is she writing down about me? Maybe I don't want actual non-Dad feedback.

When we're done, they call us to the front in

pairs to say our lines, and I'm assigned Scarecrow. As the girl playing Dorothy says her line, Ashia's words run through my mind. *And after all the shows are done, we have this incredible cast party.*

Yeah, not me, though.

I guess I channel my inner sad Scarecrow, because I don't do such a bad job with the lines. Ashia smiles from the audience, and I sort of feel bad that I haven't told her the truth yet.

Dad's already there when I get to the house. "Hi, Dad," I say, kicking off my sneakers.

"Hey, sweetie, how was your first day of school?" He's sitting on the couch with his laptop, and there's a stack of papers on the coffee table.

"It was different from having class in an airplane, but great. I met some nice kids." I drop my backpack on the bench in the entryway. "Why are you home so early?"

I try to focus on him, but the packed suitcase on the floor gets my attention instead.

"Oh, that's nothing to worry about, Kenzie," says Dad. "Last-minute trip for the weekend, but I found you a chaperone. You can stay here since you have school tomorrow."

The thing is, after only a few days in Las Vegas, I find myself missing being on the go a little. Plus, I haven't been away from my dad for a whole weekend in three years.

"I'd rather go with you, if that's okay." I sit down next to Dad and put my head on his shoulder. "It's not like I have any plans this weekend."

Dad pats my leg. "Well, I'm not sure it's the best idea to already be missing a day of school, but I know you'll make up the work," he says. "I just figured you might want to have a playdate with your new friends."

I sit up. "A playdate? Dad, I'm twelve, not five."

"Sorry, what are we calling it, then?" he asks.

But I don't even know. Hanging out? Chilling? I haven't had friends to get together with in a long time.

"It doesn't matter," I say. "Where are we going?"

"Boise," he answers.

"Good. I like Boise." I calculate the flight times in my head and plan out how long of a book to bring with me. "I'll go pack."

And as I head up the stairs, I wonder how many times I've said that same phrase in my lifetime.

chapter four

'm hanging out in the hotel room in Boise watching a movie with Genevieve, the chaperone. The Nannies to Go agency has a "thorough list" of nannies all over the country who have been "extensively screened and have excellent references." Dad tells me this every time he leaves for work, even this time, although I already know Genevieve from our other trips here. She's one of my favorites.

My phone beeps with a text from Ashia.

Where are you?! Did you get the email?!

I didn't realize I'd made such an impression in one day.

I text back.

Unexpected trip. Will be back Monday. What email?

Whoa. An all-caps text.

YOU'RE ON THE CALLBACKS LIST! THEY WANT YOU TO TRY OUT FOR THE LEAD!!!

I reread the text to make sure I understand.

I'm sorry, what now? Shelby will get the lead.

We go back and forth for at least ten minutes, but I still can't believe what she's telling me. Apparently, Shelby has made her list of demands and is already driving the teachers crazy. It's time to tell Ashia what's up.

Sorry. I can't do it. Won't be there for the performances.

Why? Out of town or something?

You could say that.

Can you be "out of town" if you're never actually *in* town?

Try anyway. You never know, right?

I put the phone down and go back to watching the movie. I'll give her all the details on Monday. It's too much to say in a text, and no one ever believes my life without a whole bunch of explanation and pictures.

An hour later, when my phone goes off again, it's another message from Ashia with Mrs. Summers's e-mail.

Let her know if you want a tryout slot! Which, OF COURSE you do.

It's kind of impossible not to be a little bit excited about this. I'm all fluttery inside as I tell Genevieve what's going on. Eventually, though, I stop and take a deep breath. "But it doesn't matter if I try out, because I won't be there for the performances," I say. I slump into the overstuffed chair.

"Although it *could* be good practice to get up onstage and conquer that fear of singing in front of people," says Genevieve. "But I do see your point. You wouldn't want to waste their time."

"Right," I say. "And my dad said we might need to stay here an extra day, which means I'd miss tryouts anyway."

"That stinks," says Genevieve.

A picture of Shelby pops into my head. "Plus, the girl who wants the lead would probably destroy me if I did audition. Apparently, she's not all that nice."

Genevieve gives me a look. "Well, don't let that stop you."

I pull my knees to my chest and remember what my mom used to say.

Don't you ever let anyone treat you like you

don't matter. Because you do. You absolutely, one hundred percent do.

I stretch my legs back out and sit up straight. "Genevieve, can I ask you something?"

She nods. "Sure."

"Is it wrong to want to hear someone besides my dad say I'm good at something?" I ask.

She smiles and scoots over next to me. "Not at all. Do you want me to weigh in? Or I could call the lunch crew up here for an impromptu concert."

I have to laugh. "Listen, I'm not saying you wouldn't tell me the truth, but you're all pretty much paid to be nice to me. Everyone around me tells me whatever they think I want to hear. Seriously, who would dare tell a VIP guest's daughter she can't sing?"

Genevieve pauses long enough to prove I'm right. And as "extensively screened" as she is, she's still a twenty-five-year-old big kid. "You know what? You're right. You need this."

But I've lost track of what we're talking about. "Wait, I need what?" I ask.

"To hear someone tell you the truth," says Genevieve. "Someone who *isn't* being paid to be nice to you."

"Or related to me," I add.

"Right, or related to you. Plus, it would be fun to see if you could get the part," she says with a mischievous grin. "Maybe teach that other girl a thing or two about show business."

I can almost see the wheels turning in her head. "But I still don't want to waste their time," I say again.

"What if you didn't?" asks Genevieve. "What if you sent a clip of you singing and they could watch it or not watch it? Their choice."

"I do have Mrs. Summers's e-mail," I say.

"And that way, if you're not there on Monday, you still get to audition." Genevieve stands up and puts her hands out in that *Why not?* kind of pose. "You could get your feedback and then politely decline if they offer you the part."

"I could do that," I say. But this is totally crazy, and I'm kind of hoping it's all just a game of "What if?" that we're playing.

Without a word, Genevieve picks up the phone and tells the concierge we need someone who can play the piano, sheet music for *The Wizard of Oz*, and a laptop. She suggests an employee at the front desk. "Have her meet us in conference room A," she says. "Oh, and make sure the piano is tuned."

I try not to abuse my hotel privileges, but it's hard not to notice that I get whatever I ask for at our hotel homes. By the time I get changed and we make it downstairs, Ava is warming up on the piano. People can make things happen pretty quickly when they want to.

Genevieve stops to chat at the concierge desk and then joins me in meeting room A.

"You can do this," she says, giving me a fist bump. "Let's see what happens, right?"

I nod. No reason to worry about standing in front of a live audience of a gazillion people (okay, maybe a few hundred), because I won't even be there for the performances. But I'm more curious than ever to hear what someone besides Dad thinks of my singing.

Ava hits the first note of "Over the Rainbow" as Genevieve starts the video on my phone.

Now or never.

I want to close my eyes and at least hide from the two people in front of me, but it always looks weird when singers don't keep their eyes open.

I can do this.

I start soft, but when it gets to the parts when I'm supposed to let loose, I do.

I actually do.

Like I'm singing in the shower. Like I'm singing in the hotel room without a care in the world.

I belt it out.

Loud.

And when I'm done, Ava stops playing and claps, but not Genevieve. Instead she's in tears.

"Was it that bad?" I ask, leaning toward her.

She steps closer and grabs my hands. "It was that good, Kenzie," she says. "It was absolutely beautiful. And I am not getting paid to say that."

Somehow I can tell she really means it. It takes me a minute to get over the shock of the compliment, but the weirdest part is that I kind of enjoyed having an audience. Even if it is a really small one.

Genevieve opens the laptop and searches for a scene we can act out. "They'll want to know you can handle lines too," she says. "I mean, if you're going to do this, do it right. You know?"

We practice our parts (this time I'm Dorothy), and it doesn't take us long to get it. Ava takes my phone, since she's now gone from front-desk clerk to pianist to videographer, as the head concierge pokes her head through the door and motions to Genevieve.

"One more thing," says Genevieve. She rushes out to the hall and comes back with a roll of gold paper. "Might as well set the scene with your very own yellow brick road."

I grab one end of the roll. "Might as well."

chapter five

always used to give my parents a hard time on Monday mornings, but now I seriously can't wait to get back to school. We didn't end up staying in Boise the extra day, so as it turns out, I'm here for the auditions. I haven't decided what I'm going to do yet, but I'm dressed, and I've already had breakfast and brushed my teeth, so I take the extra few minutes to finish unpacking.

Dad and I don't take much with us when we travel, and we only get back to our storage unit a few times a year. The last time we stopped, I grabbed my third-grade yearbook.

I take it from my bag and scan through the class pages, finding Erin and Caitlin, who I still e-mail with once in a while. The others I remember, but we've mostly lost touch, and not because I didn't try. I flip to the back, where all the group photos and school-event pictures are scattered all over the pages. The bike rodeo, field day, movie night, computer club, Spanish club. Things I never got to do in fourth grade because we left early in the school year.

A printed picture of me, Erin, and Caitlin falls from the yearbook and onto my lap. It's one of my favorites. The three of us are in Caitlin's room, huddled together on her floor, arms around one another, with our science project in front of us. We'd worked on that thing for weeks. Caitlin's walls are cotton-candy pink and covered with posters of kittens, movie stars, and all her favorite singers. Her bed is covered with fancy pillows, and an entire corner is filled with her favorite books.

I glance around my room. My temporary room. My empty, neutral-colored walls. My cream bedspread. My empty bookshelf. Really, the only things in here are my clothes in the closet, a picture of Mom in a silver frame, and a suitcase that's been to more cities than most of the kids in my class. Probably more than all of them combined.

Even the hotel rooms have more personality.

"Kenzie, time for school," Dad calls up the stairs.

"Be right down," I say back.

I grab my phone and send an e-mail to Erin and Caitlin, saying a quick "Hi! I miss you guys!" I don't even have their phone numbers to text. Actually, I don't even know if they have phones. I guess I really haven't been so great at keeping in touch. I start to close up the yearbook to put it away, but I look at the picture of the three of us one more time. A million thoughts rush through my mind.

Why can't I be a part of school activities? And why shouldn't I try new things and see what seventh grade is really like?

I might only be here for six weeks, but at least I'm here, in one spot.

Can't I cram a true middle-school experience into a month and a half? This is probably the only chance I'll ever get.

"Kenzie, time to go!" shouts Dad.

I toss the yearbook on top of the bookshelf and grab my bag for school.

"See you later, empty room," I say.

* * *

To start off my day at school, I meet the infamous Shelby with a collision in the hallway. *Ugh. Why can't I walk down a middle-school hallway without crashing into someone?*

"Hey, watch where you're going." She takes a step back and looks me up and down. "Oh. You're the new girl on the callback list."

Hmm, I've definitely never been described like that before.

"I'm Kenzie," I say. But she obviously doesn't care.

"Dorothy is *my* role," she says. The hallway crowds part around us, and Shelby stands steady. "I hope these rumors about you auditioning today aren't true, because that wouldn't be a good move."

It's not what she says that I'm afraid of—it's what she doesn't say.

I really don't want to cause trouble. I don't want to get on anyone's bad side. I'm only trying to enjoy being a regular kid for once. "I'm—" I'm about to say I'm sorry. That I'll take back my audition if it's a problem. But then I picture my yearbook full of activity photos and my empty, temporary room. And overpowering all the noise in the hallway, I hear more of my mom's words.

The pieces of advice she was determined to give me while she still could.

There are moments in life when you have to be a little bit brave and a whole lot of bold. Deep down where it counts, you'll know how.

I'm pretty sure this is one of those moments, and whether I'm ready or not, it's time to make a decision. I'll be gone in a little more than a month, and I have no intention of letting Shelby Jacobs stop me from having some fun while I'm here. "Brave and bold" is officially my new motto.

I take a deep breath and squeeze my books a little tighter. "You have a beautiful voice, Shelby. Good luck."

I walk past her with a confidence I didn't know I had, because what do I care? I won't even remember her once I'm gone.

Middle school might not have room service, free shampoo, and random celebrity sightings, but it has more activities than even most front desks can offer. Now the question is, how far can I actually get on my own, as a regular kid with no VIP privileges?

Only one way to find out.

Bren is already in his seat when I get to English, so I head right over and sit down in front of him. I slide a *very* rough draft of a poem I wrote during science class across his desk.

"Any chance you could look this over for me?" I ask. "I want to enter the poetry contest."

He picks up the paper and scans it. "What, no good morning, sunshine?"

"Good morning, sunshine," I repeat. "I also want to join book club. What do I need to do?"

I realize that joining a book club might not seem like a brave and bold move, but it's a big deal to me. The only clubs I get to be a part of are the rewards clubs at the hotels or the gold clubs for car rentals. (And, technically, my dad is the one who's the member.)

"Well, first of all, this needs some work," he says. "But it's a good start."

Wow. It's weird having someone other than Dad critique my work.

"Can you be more specific?" I ask.

Bren writes some notes in the margin, circles a few words, and adds a smiley face at the bottom. He hands it back to me.

"You know how to spell onomatopoeia?" I ask.

"Yes, Bren know how to spell," he says in a caveman voice. "And he know that onomatopoeia is word that sound like what it describe."

I laugh, loud enough to get the attention of the next row. "No, no, I don't mean it as an insult. I'm actually impressed," I say. "My dad is a spelling drill sergeant. We spent three weeks on that one before I got it."

I jot down "splash," "drip," "buzz," and "achoo" to get the onomatopoeia ideas flowing. "Wait, what's second of all?" I ask Bren.

"What?" His eyebrows angle down.

"You said 'first of all' about the poem," I say. "What's second of all?"

Mrs. Pilchard closes the door, letting us know it's time to stop talking.

Bren leans forward on his desk and whispers. "Book club meets after school on Wednesdays. Wear purple."

Having a place to sit at lunch is such a relief. Having a new nickname from Bren, not so much.

"Hello, sunshine," he says, getting right back to his book.

Ashia comes rushing over with all her usual

enthusiasm. "Are you going to do the callback?" She grabs me by the arms.

"I already did," I say. "Well, sort of. I sent Mrs. Summers a video audition."

"A video audition?" she asks. "Is that even allowed?"

"I have no idea," I answer. "But I was out of town and didn't know if I'd be here today. I'm not sure if they'll even count it." I sit down, trying to act like it's no big deal, even though it totally is. SO big. "But I'm here, so maybe I will? I don't know yet. Callbacks aren't until this afternoon, right?"

Behind me, someone is singing, and I wonder if this school might have more kids willing to put on a show in front of the whole cafeteria. Nope, definitely Tate.

But instead of just singing at his table this time, he's walking toward ours, singing "There's No Business Like Show Business."

"Is this kid for real?" I ask Ashia.

"Oh, he's the real deal," she says. "His family came here from Ireland when we were in kindergarten. It's always been rumored he was some kind of royalty."

It's not hard to picture Tate as a dashing prince.

As he sings, he gets closer and closer to our table until he's standing right in front of me. The whole room is focused on him, just like the other day, and he's eating up all the attention. But when he grabs my hand and pulls me up on the table bench, I'm convinced I'm going to pass out.

"What is he doing?" I lean down and whisper to Ashia.

She shrugs, and when the song is over, I get my answer.

"Ladies and gentlemen, please say hello to Dorothy, the lead in this year's musical!" Tate holds my hand in the air and turns me to face the rest of the room.

OH. MY. GOODNESS.

I don't know what to feel first. Shock? Happiness? Total embarrassment?

"I got the lead?" I ask Tate. "But they haven't even finished callbacks."

"Didn't need to." He jumps off the bench and gives me his hand to help me down. The chatter has picked back up as if what just happened is not the least bit strange.

"Mrs. Summers said your video blew them away," he says. "By the way, I'm Tate."

Yeah. Is there anyone in this school who doesn't know who he is?

"Have they already posted the roles?" I ask.

"Not yet," he says. "But I managed to get the inside scoop, and I had to meet you."

He had to meet me? The words run through my head as I catch a glimpse of Shelby across the room with a supervillain-got-foiled expression on her face.

"Were you supposed to announce it?" I ask. "Um, like that?"

"Don't worry. I got the okay." Tate points to the doorway, where Mrs. Summers smiles and waves before she casually turns around and heads down the hallway.

Last-week me would be freaking out right about now. TOTALLY FREAKING OUT. But the new, carefree, I'm-leaving-anyway Kenzie Rhines has a different reaction. "Oh. Thanks for delivering the message." I focus my gaze directly on Tate and smile. "You're really cute."

I expect to be utterly humiliated by the words that just came out of my mouth, but strangely, I don't care. The kid already knows he's adorable, and soon enough I'll never have to face him again.

His eyes open wide and he's silent.

This should be the part where I panic. The part where I wish I could take back what I said. But instead I wink at him.

I wink at the cutest boy in school, after telling him he's cute.

And then I laugh. Because for the first time in a long time, I'm not the least bit concerned with my next destination.

chapter six

Poetry contest. Book club. Lead in the musical. Middle school is like a buffet of activity choices. It doesn't matter if you're into music, art, sports, or books—there are a million things to do. And it's weird, because there are a million things to do everywhere I go, and Dad can pretty much get us into anything. But here it's all up to me. Only me.

I stand in front of the class council poster. SEVENTH-GRADE ELECTIONS. Hmm.

"Your boy Tate is running for class president," says the voice behind me.

I turn around and find Bren chewing on a

piece of licorice. "Is that breakfast?" I ask, ignoring his comment.

"Are you planning on running for something?" he asks, ignoring my question. I'm not even sure it's an actual conversation at this point.

"That's not healthy." I decide there's no reason to answer that last one, either.

"You should run," he says. "About time someone other than Golden Boy gets everything."

I don't know much about anyone here yet, but I'm not surprised to hear that Tate does it all. "Are you running?"

Bren shakes his head as the warning bell rings for homeroom. "See Mrs. Pilchard if you're interested. The deadline to get your name on the ballot is Friday."

I have no intention of putting my name on that ballot, although it does sound interesting.

As soon as Bren walks away, Ashia catches me looking at the poster. "Are you thinking of running?" she asks.

We walk toward our homerooms through the crowd of students. "Me? No. Just trying to stay informed," I say.

"It's a great idea," she says. "I'm awesome at organizing, and I have a bunch of friends in art club who could help with posters. It would be fun."

Everything she's saying sounds kind of amazing, but running for class president would really be pushing it. It's a yearlong commitment I wouldn't even come close to finishing.

We're at my stop. "From what I hear, Tate will win it anyway," I say, trying to talk my way out of this.

Ashia stands firm. "You might be exactly what this school needs, Kenzie Rhines. Fresh ideas. A new take on things. A girl with a plan."

"But I don't have a plan," I say.

"Come to my house after school." She slinks away before I can argue. "We'll make one."

Musical rehearsals don't start until next week and book club isn't until tomorrow, so after school I get the okay from Dad and walk home with Ashia.

"Ashia, I love your enthusiasm, but I am not running for class president," I say, lounging in the papasan chair in her bedroom. It's a total middle-school girl bedroom with purple walls and posters all over the place. It definitely beats my bland walls. "I'm not even president material."

"You are what you believe you are," says Ashia, waving a hand in the air like she's a spiritual guru.

"I have a question," I say. "Why aren't *you* running for class president? You'd be amazing at it."

"Um, no," says Ashia, flipping open a notebook.

"Why not?" I ask. "You participate in a million things, everyone likes you, and you said yourself that you're great at organizing."

She's silent, which I take as a sign to keep going. "You're super friendly, you seem pretty smart, and you have great ideas. I mean, other than your idea of *me* running for president. That was a bad one."

She smiles. "You really think I'd make a good class president?"

"I really do," I say.

Ashia bites her lip and plays with the tassel on one of her bright-pink pillows. After a minute or so of what seems to be some intense thinking, she takes a deep breath and exhales slowly.

"Okay, I'll do it," she finally says. "But on one condition."

"And what's that?" I ask. "You want me to run your campaign? That could be fun."

Ashia scoots to the corner of her bed so she's

sitting right in front of me. "No, I want you to be my vice president."

I laugh, until I see the look on her face. "Wait, you're serious?"

"Of course I'm serious," she says. "Think of all the fun we'd have."

And I do. For one glorious minute, I think about all the things Ashia and I could do together as a team. *If* I were going to actually be here to do it.

"I can't."

"Well, then I'm not doing it either," she says. "It won't be any fun without you."

I adjust as much as I can in the papasan. "I don't think the point of it is necessarily to have fun. You're supposed to want to do good for your class and make changes that will improve their school experience," I say.

Ashia stares at me. "See what I mean?" she says. "You're a freaking natural at this. Listen, Kenzie, I think I really want to do this. All those things you just said convinced me. But I need you. I can't win this thing without you by my side. Please?"

Oh man, this is tough. I finally have a friend I love hanging out with, and she's asking me for a favor. One tiny favor that wouldn't make a lick of difference to me, but that would make the rest of her school year awesome.

"Pretty please?" she says when I don't respond.

Maybe I actually could help her make some changes for the good of the class while I'm here. I'd have at least a few weeks "in office" to get things done. And I can't imagine it would be all that hard to find a replacement seventh-grade vice president. Although I thought schools did this differently.

"Wait, don't they elect a class president and vice president separately?" I ask.

She smiles like she can tell I'm softening up. "Most schools do," she says. "But Mr. Kumar thinks it's important to mirror the way it's done in the real world. So the president chooses her running mate."

"Well, that makes sense," I say. "Except I doubt middle-school kids are choosing the most qualified person for the job. They're picking their friends."

Ashia laughs. "Yeah, pretty much. So, not *quite* like the real world." She hugs the pillow on her lap. "Come on, you and me. What do you say?"

I think it all through one more time. All the

reasons I absolutely should not agree to this, and all the reasons that maybe I should.

"Okay, let's do it," I say.

Ashia jumps off the bed with a squeal and gives me a gigantic hug. She's surprisingly strong. And in this moment, while I'm not really sure I made the right choice, I do know that I picked the right friend.

"Now let's see what qualifications you have so we can start a list." Ashia gets out a piece of paper and a pencil from her desk drawer. "What positions did you have in your other school?"

It's the first time the subject has come up, and I'm torn between telling her the truth and keeping up with my very vague background story. But one thing I know for sure is that telling her I'm leaving in less than six weeks will stop this mission in its tracks—and maybe even this friendship. I can't take that chance.

"Um, line leader?" I say.

Ashia laughs. "No, seriously. Anything official? Any clubs in sixth grade we can list?"

Yeah, frequent-flier clubs.

"I wasn't all that involved in school activities last year," I say.

"Okay, not a problem. How about things outside

of school?" she asks. "Dance? Book clubs? Group activities?"

I sit up straight. This one I've got. "Well, I danced with the Chicago Ballet once. And once I got to fill in for a townsperson in a Broadway musical. I mean, I didn't have any lines, but still. Ooh, and I got to assist the stage crew at a Maroon Five concert."

It's not until Ashia's jaw drops and her eyes practically pop out that it dawns on me how *not* normal all of that sounds.

"Did you really do all that?" she asks.

This totally could go either way, but I decide to let her in on a little snippet of my world. "I really did. My dad has a ton of connections."

"Do you have pictures of all that?" she asks.

I nod.

"See, now we have a plan," she says. "People are going to eat this up. What else you got?"

We spend the next hour with me telling stories of my adventures and her writing down the best parts. I'm careful not to give too many details and to make sure I mention regular things like home-work and cleaning my room. I don't mention it's hotel housekeeping that does that for me.

"Can I ask you something?" she says, but it's only

the polite intro to what comes next. "Is it just . . . you and your dad?"

I run through all the stories I've told her today. I never said my mom wasn't around anymore, but it's painfully clear since she's not a part of any of them. "Yeah."

She waits, as everyone always does, because how do you ever know if it's okay to ask?

I sit on the edge of the chair, hug one of her throw pillows, and stare down at my feet. "You know how sometimes there's a really horrible flu that goes around and on the news they casually mention that a couple people died of complications from it, but you don't pay much attention because, well, it's a couple people and you don't know who they are?"

I turn my gaze toward Ashia and she nods.

"One of those people was my mom," I say, kicking my feet back and forth. "She got a bad infection and they couldn't . . ." It doesn't matter how long it's been; it's still the hardest thing in the world to say those words.

Ashia leans forward and puts her hand on mine. "It's okay, Kenzie. You don't have to tell me all of it. I'm so sorry." And then she says something I wish more people did. Something people are afraid to say, but that can be the absolute best thing in the world for a girl who misses her mother. "Tell me something about her?"

I look up and smile, slowly. "She loved to ice-skate," I say. It's the first memory that pops into my mind. "I was never very good, but she'd take me all the time."

Ashia goes over to her bookshelf and picks up a trophy. "I like to skate too," she says, handing it to me.

"Wow. You figure-skate?" I ask.

"Sort of. I gave it up this year to do more at school, but if you want, we could go together sometime. I mean, if that's something you'd want to do."

"I'd like that," I say, releasing my grip on the pillow.

Ashia sits down on the bed, close to where I am in the chair. "Will you tell me more about her? I bet she was amazing." This time she smiles, and when she does, I get this swirl of gratefulness through my whole body. I forgot what it was like to have a friend to talk to.

"She was the most amazing," I say.

chapter seven

As I'm walking to book club the next day after school, Ashia calls down the hall.

"Kenzie, wait up!" she shouts.

She's been talking about our campaign every time we're together, but I'm still not convinced I should run. I mean, it would be beyond awesome to win it, but I can't stop thinking that I won't be here to *be* vice president.

"We totally need to get buttons," she says, catching up to me.

"Buttons?" I ask. We stop in front of the library entrance, and she hands me a piece of paper. A flyer. Our election flyer, apparently.

"Madison Yencer did the design. What do you

think?" She doesn't wait for an answer. "So we can take the logo with our names and put it on buttons and get them around the school to start drumming up support. But we have to hurry; otherwise, rush processing will cost a fortune."

I stand there, stunned.

"I'll take that as your okay." She takes the flyer back and puts it inside a folder labeled OFFICIAL CAMPAIGN INFO. "Oh, I need a picture of us for promotional purposes." She takes out her phone and squeezes in next to me for a selfie. "Smile."

Imagining our election flyers all over the school snaps me out of my trance. "Ashia, I can't."

"Sure you can. Now smile!" I do as she asks to at least get past this hurdle. "Perfect," she says.

I repeat my resistance to her plan. "I really can't do it. I should have told you before, but I won't be here."

She tilts her head to the side. "Is that seriously your excuse for getting out of everything?"

It's time to tell her. This is getting out of control. *Spit it out, Kenzie.*

"It's the truth: I won't be around to be your vice president." But apparently I'm not clear enough.

"Listen, Kenzie," she says. "I know you and your

dad go on your weekend jaunts or whatever, but all your official duties will be during the week. A Friday night here and there, but it won't be a problem. I'm the one who needs to be here for all the events. I'm telling you, we can totally win this thing."

I stop and take in her words. She thinks we can win. I guess there really is only one way to find out. But am I up for it?

"Okay," I say.

Ashia pumps her fist with a silent *yes!*

At that moment, Bren sticks his head into the hallway. "Kenzie, you coming to book club or what?"

"I'll be right there," I say. As he's about to duck back into the library, I grab his purple sleeve. "Hey, why are we wearing purple?"

His eyebrows go up, and his face practically glows. "Matches the book cover. Genius, right? Totally my idea."

When he disappears, I shake my head. "I'm not sure I've ever met someone like that boy."

"Definitely not," says Ashia. And before I even turn to head into the library, she's off down the hall. "I'll see you later. I need to order the buttons!"

* * *

On Thursday morning, Ashia signs up to run for president and I submit my name to Mrs. Pilchard for seventh-grade vice president. Thursday night, Ashia's mom takes us shopping for the perfect Election Day outfits.

After school on Friday, I finish up an assignment and decide to check my e-mail. Not that there's ever anything there, but I cross my fingers as I click on the inbox.

And there it is—an e-mail from Erin and Caitlin. I didn't realize how much I missed them until I finally stopped and let the world spin around me without me spinning along with it.

I e-mail them back and type their numbers in my phone. I know kids these days text, but I plan on calling them next week instead. Because it dawns on me that I don't even remember what their voices sound like.

And just as I'm deciding against texts, I get one from Ashia inviting me to stay over and work on election stuff.

I'm thrilled when Dad says I can sleep over at Ashia's. I quickly pack a few changes of clothes for our "photo shoot." You'd think I wouldn't want to sleep anywhere else now that I have one place to have my things and my very own bed. But the thought of a sleepover makes my insides feel like they're at a New Year's Eve party.

"Are you sure you're okay with this, Dad?" I ask. "You won't be lonely?"

Dad laughs and pulls me in for a hug. "Kenzie, you are quite possibly the sweetest preteen on the planet, you know that? I'll be fine. You go have fun."

I smile and lift the strap of my bag over my shoulder. "Okay. If you're sure."

"I'm sure," says Dad.

Ashia's mom pulls into the driveway, and I give Dad another hug before I head out the door.

"Don't stay up too late!" he shouts from the doorway. "Kidding. Stay up as late as you want."

Maybe it's not Dad I'm worried about. Maybe I'm the one who isn't sure how to spend a night away from him. The days I'm used to, but I always have Dad to let me know everything's okay every night before I go to bed—no matter where we are.

"Helloooo." Ashia is waving her hand in front of my face. I shake my head to get out of my trance as we pull into their driveway.

"We're here already?" I ask.

"I only live a few blocks from you, silly girl," says Ashia.

We go straight to the kitchen for all the goodies Mrs. Boyce has ready for us. There's chocolate-covered something-or-others (does it matter?), popcorn, and all kinds of fruit I can't even identify. Star fruit? Guava, maybe? Isn't there something called dragon fruit?

We each make a plate of food; then we head into the living room and sit on the floor, using the coffee table as both our snack table and our desk. Ashia already has all the election info out.

"We need some really standout photos for the posters to catch everyone's attention," she says. "We should think outside the box and be different."

We're quiet for a few minutes, except for the crunching of popcorn.

"Maybe we could come up with something fun to do at school," I say. "Like things you can do to be part of the group." A chance to be part of a group is definitely something I'd notice.

"Yeah, I like where you're going with this," says Ashia, popping a grape in her mouth.

"We could have an ice-skating get-together with hot chocolate after and call it 'Breaking the

Ice,' so kids who don't know each other can meet up and chat." It's possible I'm channeling my need to do these things, but I figure I can't be the only one who feels that way, even if my circumstances are pretty different.

"That's a great idea!" Ashia writes it down on her list.

"And we could have a day each month where students get to do their favorite things," I continue. "Like wearing pajamas to school and having pizza for lunch."

"Pizza and pj's," says Ashia. "I love it! See, I totally need you for this."

Although, if anything, I'd only make it to one Pizza and Pj's Day.

"Do you think Mr. Kumar would even allow that?" I ask.

"Sure. We've done silly things like that before. But we can make it a regular thing," she says. "Now if we can get him to let us do a Use Your Cell Phone Day, we'd win this thing no contest." She winks, although I think it's a fantastic idea.

We spend the next two hours brainstorming and then have her mom take pictures of us: in our cutest pj's (okay, so mine are actually Ashia's that she let me borrow) holding a pizza box, dressed up in winter coats and hats and ice skates (she has an old pair in my size), one in patriotic colors, and, for what will possibly be our most popular idea, texting on our phones.

When we're sufficiently wiped out, we crash on Ashia's bed.

"Thanks for inviting me over," I say.

"Of course." Ashia kicks off her slippers. "That's what friends are for."

That one little statement makes me happier than I've been in a long time.

"I haven't had a sleepover in forever," I say. "What's next?"

Ashia sits up and counts each item on her fingers. "Well, for starters, we need to do each other's hair and nails. And it is not officially a sleepover if you don't gossip about boys, so there's that. We can watch a movie, and of course hop on social media."

I laugh, thinking how Ashia is like a sleepover concierge, arranging activities for her guests.

"We better get started, then." I grab a brush out of my bag. "Who goes first?"

"Oh, Kenzie," she says. "You can't brush my hair with that kind of brush."

"No?" I ask, clueless.

"I would be a frizzy mess," she answers. "So I guess the first thing we're doing is a lesson on curly-girl hair."

Her stance with her hand on her hip makes me giggle. See, this is the kind of stuff I don't learn on the road.

chapter eight

love these pictures," says Ashia.

Bren looks over her shoulder at the photo on my phone and narrates its description. "Kenzie Rhines and Ashia Boyce, hanging out in their pajamas and eating—" Bren pauses. "Ooh, what kind of pizza is that?"

"Veggie," says Ashia. "My mom insists I get my veggies with each meal."

"Doesn't the tomato sauce count?" asks Bren.

"Nope," answers Ashia. "Because it's still under debate whether a tomato is a vegetable or a fruit."

We all nod, like it's the most interesting thing we've heard all day. Actually, it probably is.

"I can tell you where the best pizza is," I say. "I've tried a ton of them. Although it depends if you like deep-dish like Chicago or thin-crust like New York City. But my personal favorites are San Francisco, Philly, Buffalo, and San Diego."

Ashia smiles because she knows I've been all over, but Bren is staring at me like I'm an alien.

"You've had pizza in all those places?" he asks.

Words form in my mind, but I can't seem to get the right sentences together to explain it without giving anything away.

"She travels with her dad on the weekends for work," says Ashia.

I'm trying desperately to let school be a place where no one knows about my VIP status, but I'm not doing such a great job. "Yeah, for work" is all I say.

As I take the phone back from Ashia, someone else is looking over my shoulder.

"Hey, Dorothy," says Tate. "Can I talk to you?"

Annoying Bren makes a kissy face at me, and I shoot my best *don't mess with me* look back at him.

I walk out to the hall with Tate, wondering if he saw the picture.

"Listen, I expect competition for president, but I'm kind of surprised to see that it's you and Ashia," he says, tucking a piece of hair behind his ear.

"Why is that?" I ask. He'd better not say it's because we're girls.

"It's just that I'm really looking forward to getting to know you," he says. "And maybe competing against each other isn't the best thing right now."

What he's saying is ridiculous, I know this. But those eyes are staring at me like they're smiling and dancing and shooting out rainbows all at the same time. *Get it together, Kenzie.*

"You'd be a great secretary," he says, knocking me out of his stare trance.

I square my shoulders and stand tall. "I'd also be a great *vice president*," I say back.

"Yeah, yeah, of course," he says, shifting from one foot to the other. "I'm just saying that if I was president and you were secretary or treasurer, we'd get to work together. We'd be spending a lot of time with each other between that and the musical. Wouldn't that be awesome?" He smiles and quite possibly lights up the hallway.

OMG, he's so freaking adorable that I am *almost* tempted to agree with him. Luckily, my bold and brave side takes over.

"You want us to work together?" I ask.

"It would be so great." He takes a step closer and puts a hand on my shoulder.

When the tingles shoot through me, I move my shoulder enough to make his hand drop. "Then I suggest *you* run for secretary," I say. "See you at rehearsal."

Based on his shocked expression, I'm guessing most girls give in to his charms.

But I am definitely not most girls.

When Dad gets home, I want to tell him all about rehearsal. How I stood onstage in front of everyone and recited my lines. I even want to tell him about Tate—the cute boy who both makes my heart beat faster and makes me wonder what the heck I'm thinking. I want to tell him about the election and the posters and even the buttons. But I can't.

So when he asks what I've been up to at school, I casually mention helping with the musical and focus more on what we're reading for book club.

"That sounds fun," he says from his end of the dinner table. "It's not a problem that we're leaving in a month?"

I shove a big bite of pizza in my mouth so I have time to think about my answer. I shake my head and change the topic as I mentally add Las Vegas pizza to my favorites. Yum.

"I was thinking that since we're in one place for a bit, I could try some new things," I say, picking a piece of pineapple off the pizza and popping it in my mouth. "And maybe work on getting better at some things I haven't done in a while."

"Like what?" asks Dad.

"Like ice-skating."

Dad looks down at the table for only a second, and I know what he's thinking.

"Ashia said she'd take me. You don't have to." I grab my plate and move over to sit beside him. It's moments like these that are both extra hard and smile-worthy at the same time, because without a doubt, we're both picturing Mom gliding around the ice. "And also photography. I'd like to take a class or something and join the photography club at school."

Dad puts his hand on mine. "That all sounds great, Kenzie. Let me know what you need."

My phone beeps, letting me know I have a text. Probably Ashia with a button update.

Hey there. Sorry about earlier. Forgive me?

I don't recognize the number, but I see that it's a Las Vegas area code.

Forgive you for what? Also, who is this?

The little dots on my screen let me know the mystery texter is writing something.

Tate

Oh. Well, at least in a text I don't have to look at him and get distracted. I write back.

Have you decided to concede? ;)

As soon as I send it, I regret going the playful route. I should be giving this kid the wrath of an angry middle-school girl.

No way. I look forward to running against such strong opponents.

Oh man, why'd he have to go and be all charming again? I answer with a thumbs-up emoticon, and as soon as I send it, my phone rings.

"Hello?"

"Hi, it's Bren."

"Oh, I didn't think kids actually called each other anymore," I say. "How'd you get my phone number?" *And on that note, how did Tate get my number?*

"They don't, but it's a lost art," says Bren.

I totally agree, and make myself a note to make those phone calls to Erin and Caitlin this week.

"Are you free tomorrow after school?" asks Bren.

I have no idea what's going on right now. Tate sort of apologized (wait, that wasn't technically an apology, was it?) and now Bren is . . . He's not asking me out, is he?

"You still there, Kenzie?" he asks.

"Oh yeah, I—I'm here," I stutter out. "Why, what's going on tomorrow?" I ask.

"Well, like it or not, Ashia has deemed me your campaign manager."

"You're our campaign manager?" I ask, with maybe a little too much sarcasm.

"As I said, like it or not."

"Okay, no, this is good," I say. "I'm sure you're very organized and have a lot of good ideas." Look on the bright side, right?

"Nope. I am neither organized nor full of ideas," he says. "But I do know how to win you guys this position."

I have to admit, I'm curious. "And how are you going to do that?" I ask.

"You know, we could have been off the phone ages ago if you'd answered my first question," he says. "Are you free tomorrow? I'll explain everything then."

"Ages ago? We've been on for two minutes," I say.

"And yes, I'm free. There's no musical rehearsal until Thursday."

"Good. See you in school tomorrow, and we can meet up in the library at dismissal," he says. "Bren out."

I'm shaking my head when I hear the call disconnect. Did he really say "Bren out" and hang up?

Hotel employees are so much more pleasant than middle-school boys.

chapter nine

When I get to the library after school, Bren and Ashia are already there. Unfortunately, so is Shelby, and she's standing in the doorway with a gaggle of chatty friends.

"Oh hey, Kenzie," she says with what I'm convinced is an evil cackle. "Looks like you're going all out, huh? The lead in the musical *and* class vice president? You think you can handle it?"

This girl gets under my skin like no one ever has, but at the same time, I feel sorry for her. She has no clue what it means to be a decent human being.

"Don't forget book club. I do that, too." I

squeeze past her and tell myself not to look back. Although I'm hoping the expression on her face is an extremely annoyed one.

The table in front of Bren and Ashia is covered with papers, including mock-ups of election posters.

"Madison put these together for us, and we're trying to narrow it down to two," says Ashia, pushing the small versions of the posters in front of me.

I take a minute to study them, still not fully able to believe I'm doing this. "This one." I point to one of me and Ashia all decked out in red, white, and blue that Madison added a White House background to. "And this one." Because we have to promote our pizza and pj's idea.

"My favorites as well," says Bren. "It appears we have much more in common than you'd think," he says with a smile.

"What's next?" I ask.

Bren goes over a list of things we need to get done, and we split up all the tasks among the three of us. I have to admit we work pretty well together. It takes hardly any time at all, since we agree on almost every point.

And then . . . Shelby's back. She picks up one of the posters, tilts it from side to side, and puts it back on the table. "My mom works at a printing shop. I could get these done for you if you want."

Ashia and I exchange *What the heck is happening right now?* looks.

"What?" says Shelby. "I'm not the evil witch you guys think I am."

Well, this is awkward.

"Plus, I need a favor," she says. *Ah, there it is.* "Tate listens to you. Put in a good word for me and I'll do your posters."

Shelby likes Tate? Oh man. I should have figured.

"I don't know if I can do that," I say.

And just like that, somewhat-sweet Shelby disappears. "Is it really that hard to think of something nice to say about me? Seriously, Kenzie?"

Um, yeah, it is.

"I just . . . I mean . . . I don't think I want to get in the middle of whatever this is," I say, fumbling over my words. I can't tell her there's a slight chance that *I* might possibly like Tate. Maybe.

Shelby looks like she's about to explode when Ashia steps in to save the day. "I'll do it," she says. "I've known Tate forever."

Shelby's shoulders relax, and she gives Ashia a huge (fake) grin. "Perfect. E-mail me the photos. I'll have the posters done in a couple days." And with that, she pivots on her heel and walks out of the library, her shoulders bouncing with each step.

Once she's gone, Bren gets his things together, stands up, and slings his bag over his shoulder. "Girls are weird" is all he says before doing a pivot imitation of Shelby and sauntering out of the library.

My dad didn't exactly sign me up for photography *class*. He surprises me with the news when we get to Washington, DC, on Saturday.

"I thought a lesson from a real pro would be invaluable," says Dad. "We went to college together, and now he's one of the most sought-after photographers. Plus, he's really looking forward to meeting you."

"Dad, I meant a class in Vegas. You know, like normal kids take?" We walk along the reflecting pool toward the Lincoln Memorial. It's one of my favorite places in the world.

"I know, but this is better, don't you think?" He stops, and I nod in agreement. It's not like VIP privileges aren't awesome, and I'm kind of glad I still get to have them on the weekends. When we get to the steps leading up to the enormous statue of Lincoln, we sit down. "I have something for you," says Dad.

He takes a gift bag out of the big tote he's been carrying. "Open it," he says.

I pull out the tissue paper and find a black camera bag and unzip it to find a brand-new camera inside. "This is for me?" I ask.

He chuckles and puts an arm around me. "Yes, it's for you. I'm so proud of how well you're doing in school. And you're so brave to try out new things," he says. "When you said you wanted to learn photography, I thought it made sense for you to have your own camera."

I turn the camera on, point it at the reflecting pool, and snap a picture. "You know, Dad, we go so many fun places, I really should start taking pictures with something other than my phone." I check out the image on the screen. Not too bad, I guess.

Dad gives my shoulder a squeeze. "Kuan-yin should be here any minute," he says.

A slim man with photography equipment slung over his shoulder walks up the steps toward us as a girl about my age follows behind him.

"Brian," says the man I'm assuming is Kuan-yin.

"It's been too long," says Dad, and they give each other a big hug, complete with pats on the back. "And who is this?"

"This is my daughter, Mayleen." He puts a hand on her arm and a proud smile on his face. "And you must be Kenzie."

We all exchange hellos and move out of the way as a big group of tourists heads for the statue.

"We should let the dads catch up," says Mayleen. She doesn't give me a chance to answer, just grabs my arm and directs me up the stairs.

"Yeah, okay then." I move right along with her until we get to the walls of the memorial.

"This is my favorite part," she says. "Everyone goes for the reflecting pool or the statue, but this . . ." She stops and faces the back wall. "Did you know this cost three million dollars to build?"

"I didn't," I say. "But I do know that two presidents and Lincoln's only surviving son were here for the dedication in 1922. My dad includes Abraham Lincoln facts in any lesson he can, and if I'm being honest, I love it."

"This is my favorite part of all." She points up and reads. "'In this temple, as in the hearts of the

people for whom he saved the Union, the memory
of Abraham Lincoln is enshrined forever.'"

It's not easy finding twelve-year-old history
buffs. I like this girl. "You're kind of awesome," I say.

"Kind of?" she replies with a smile. "You don't
know the half of it."

I laugh as Dad and Kuan-yin come back to
where we're standing. "Are you ready for your lesson?" asks Dad.

I nod and pat my shiny new camera.

For the next two hours, the four of us walk
all over DC. Kuan-yin gives me tips on lighting,
camera angles, and perspective. And it turns out
Mayleen is a photography guru herself. When we
get to the White House lawn (or at least the fence
in front of the White House lawn), the dads sit
down for a rest (older people have to do that, I
guess) while Mayleen and I go take a million photos of ourselves in front of the most famous house
in the country. I mean, how can we not end the day
with a White House selfie?

"Why haven't we ever met before?" asks
Mayleen.

"My dad and I travel a lot," I say. "Like all the
time. Seriously."

"So where's home?" she asks.

"Good question," I say. "Hotels are my home."

"No way. That's so incredibly cool."

"It is, most of the time. But we're staying in Las Vegas for six weeks and I'm kind of loving middle school," I say. "Is that weird?"

She lets out a giggle. "Oh man, Kenzie, if I could travel all the time and not go to middle school, I'd be all over that."

"The grass is always greener on the other side of the fence, right?" I say.

"Very true." Mayleen hands me her phone. "Put your number in. We *have* to stay in touch."

I punch in my number and add my name with "White House Selfie Extraordinaire" as my business name. "Next time we're in Washington, we are so hanging out," I say.

We walk back to the dads, who are now rested, and when they inform us that we're all having dinner together, I couldn't be happier. Even though I feel like I'm living two completely different lives right now (one normal and one not so much), they somehow go really well together.

chapter ten

When I get to school on Monday, people are everywhere, hanging election posters up.

Ashia runs over to me with two big rolls of tape in her hands. "See why we needed to come in early?" she says, looking annoyed. "We have to get the best poster spots."

Madison, the girl who designed our flyers, is looking even more frantic than Ashia. "I got you guys the front display case and the gym doors, but I lost the library bulletin board. I'm so sorry." Before I can even respond, she has already taken off, and is putting up a poster on the front of a water fountain.

I didn't take it seriously when Ashia texted me last night, but I guess I really shouldn't have hit snooze on my alarm this morning. Tate is over by the office doors, getting a good setup for his poster.

I grab one of the rolls of tape. "Where are the posters?" She leads me to two stacks of them, courtesy of Shelby, who really did come through for us. "Did you honor your end of the deal?" I ask Ashia.

"Sure did," she says. "I mentioned to Tate that Shelby was very helpful with our campaign and can't she be the sweetest thing sometimes?"

"What did he say?" I ask.

"He laughed at me. Thought I was joking around," she says. "But I did my part. Here's your pile." She hands me some posters, and I take off to the office, where I line up our poster right next to Tate's.

"What are you doing?" he asks. "This is my spot."

I smooth it down around the edges. "Yes, and this"—I point to the poster I've put up—"is my spot."

He gives me a smirk. "Too bad you're new around here and don't know all the best places."

His poster looks great. Mainly because his face takes up most of it. If only he weren't so freaking cute.

But I let myself get distracted for too long, and Tate is already down the hall. Probably getting those coveted spots I don't know about.

"Don't listen to him." Bren walks up next to me. "Poster placement isn't what's going to win this thing."

We walk down by the main bulletin boards and I put up another one, as Bren hands out buttons to students passing by. It's a frenzy of activity with everyone battling for prime poster locations. Two students going in different directions slam into each other right near us. We help them up and Bren gives them each a button, never missing an opportunity.

"Why don't they let students put the posters up before this week?" I ask. "This is out of control."

"Well, there was an incident last year," he says.

We walk down the hall as Bren points to another place to hang posters. "What kind of incident?" I ask. Someone in the distance is ripping a poster off the wall and clearly causing a problem. "Worse than this?"

"Oh yeah," says Bren. "Way worse."

When he doesn't tell me more, I take the bag of buttons out of his hands. "What happened?"

But we're interrupted by Ashia. "Hey, we only have five more minutes. Enough with the chitchat." She hands me more posters and says, "Social studies hallway," before heading in the other direction.

"You owe me a story," I say to Bren. And even though you're not supposed to run in the hallways, I do. Because I'm not quite sure yet which is worse—having to face the principal or having to deal with Ashia if these posters don't get up in time.

As if the craziness of the morning weren't enough, there's musical rehearsal after school, and we're working on one of my solos.

Oh boy.

I've been shaking since the last period of the day and can't seem to get myself together. I'm backstage in a little corner, counting down the minutes and trying desperately to calm myself down.

"You can do this, Kenzie," I say out loud. "It's like singing in the hotel rooms. Sort of. Not really."

I must have missed the footsteps behind me, but I catch Tate's voice loud and clear.

"You can definitely do this," he says. And for the first time, I notice a small hint of that faded Irish accent. "You okay?"

I'm fairly certain my cheeks have turned the color of the Smell the Roses red crayon I used in art class earlier. I let out a slow breath. "I'm really nervous."

He pulls earbuds out of his pocket, attaches them to his phone, and taps the screen, then finally hands everything over to me. "Here. Give yourself a minute—you'll be fine."

I put the earbuds in and Judy Garland's voice takes over. I lean back against the tile wall, slide down to the floor, and close my eyes, totally immersed in the music. When the song is over, I open my eyes. Tate is sitting right next to me.

I pull the headphones out and hand everything back to him. "Thank you for that."

"Sometimes you need to be focused on something else," he says. "You ready?"

I nod, not sure if I actually am. He gets up first, extends a hand to help me up, and doesn't let go as we walk to the front.

"You've got this, Kenzie," he says. "I'll be sitting in the front row."

I let go of his hand. The last thing I need right now is to be nervous about him, too. "Why are you helping your competition?" I ask.

He smiles. "You're not my competition here. Only on the campaign trail." Tate glides down the stairs, leaving me standing in the middle of the stage. The whole cast is sitting behind the directors, and even the stage crew has filed into the auditorium seats. As promised, Tate is sitting front and center.

You wanted this, I remind myself. *Now take your best shot.*

I close my eyes and picture Judy Garland herself up on this stage, singing her heart out. I imagine sparkly red shoes on my feet and a tiny little dog in my arms. When the pianist plays the first note, I open my mouth to sing . . . and can't remember a single word.

"Are you okay, Kenzie?" asks the director, after a long, uncomfortable pause.

But I can't even answer her. Everyone is watching me. The room is silent.

It is without a doubt my biggest opportunity for a bold and brave moment.

But this time, I run offstage and fail miserably.

chapter eleven

t's not that bad," says Ashia at lunch the next day.

"It's that bad," I respond, plopping my head into my arms on the table. The rest of the girls at the table try to console me, but Bren has other ideas, apparently.

"She doesn't need you to lie to her," he says. "What she needs is some strategies to beat this stage fright."

I silently take his words under advisement.

"You've got a lot to learn about girls, Bren," says Ashia. "Sometimes we just need our girl-friends to make us feel better, even if it is a lie."

I pop my head up. "So it really is as bad as I think it is? Oh man, I'm doomed."

Ashia wraps an arm around me. "I'm so sorry, Kenzie. We'll figure this out. We'll find you a way to get past this."

Bren puts his hands out, palms up. "Isn't that what I said?"

Ashia shakes her head at him and gives him a *not now, Bren* look. Although I was thinking the same thing he was.

"How about something to take your mind off it?" asks Bren. He faces Ashia. "Is that a girl thing or no?"

She doesn't respond to his sarcasm.

"What did you have in mind?" I ask.

"We're starting a new book tomorrow for book club, and I was thinking that since it's about different cultures coming together, we could have sort of an international feast," he says. "Brilliant or what?"

I certainly don't want to call Bren brilliant, but it is a great idea. And planning a party might take my mind off things. That is, if I can make it through today's rehearsal. "That sounds good. Do you want me to text everyone?"

"Yes, please," he says. "They can complain to *you* that it's so last-minute." He gives me a sinister smile, like it's what he planned all along. But I won't give him the satisfaction of knowing he got me.

"What color are we wearing?" I ask. "The book cover is mostly brown, right?"

He smiles again, but this time it's a plain old happy smile. "You're really getting the hang of this place, huh, sunshine?"

And while my stage-fright disaster might suggest otherwise, I have to agree with him. For the first time in a long time, I might actually be fitting in.

I'm hiding in the back row of the auditorium, sending out a group text to book-club members, when a crazy thought hits me.

I have enough friends to group message.

In most twelve-year-old lives, this probably isn't such a big deal, but to me, it's huge. When a text notification goes off, I get ready for complaints. But instead it's a really nice surprise.

Hey, Kenzie! It's Mayleen. How are things?

I have to ignore it at first because a book-club text comes through. And another one. I finally type a response to Mayleen.

Not good. Ran offstage at practice yesterday.

Another text comes through, so I try to catch

up. Everyone seems to have a reason they can't do the feast.

Not enough time to get it ready.

Parents are busy tonight.

Can't pick a food.

Really, people? This shouldn't be so difficult. I respond with It was Bren's idea and get a bunch of Ah, that makes more sense texts back. Surprisingly, they all jump on board. As irritating as Bren is, people seem to love him. The next one is from Mayleen.

Oh man. That's rough.

Right?

So sing to me next time.

Huh?

Sing to me. FaceTime me when you go up there. Put the phone where you can see me.

What makes you so sure I won't be TOTALLY embarrassed singing to you?

Don't worry. I have a plan.

K is all I text back. The girl has a *you can trust me* kind of face.

"Kenzie, can I talk to you for a minute?" Mrs. Summers, the head director, is standing at the end of the row.

"Sure." I put away my phone as she scoots into the seat next to me.

"It can be really hard to get up there in front of everyone," she says. "And we're happy to work through it with you. We can talk about some strategies to use."

I nod and let her keep talking.

"I just need to know that you're committed to this," she says. "If you're in it for the long haul, so are we."

UGH. Just when I've semiforgotten my secret agenda, someone slaps me in the face with it. It's either nerves or guilt creeping its way through my arms right now, but neither one is a good option. I consider telling her—I do. I mean, to be honest, backing out of this thing right now would solve a whole bunch of problems for me. But then I'll always be the girl who ran offstage and couldn't do it. And I don't want to be that girl.

"I'm in, Mrs. Summers," I say. "Kenzie Rhines is not a quitter." At least I don't think she is. I've never actually had anything like this to quit before.

She smiles as she gets up, and the seat bottom clunks back and forth against the hard metal

back. "Great. You're on in five, but we'll do a group
number today to ease you into it."

When I pull out my phone, there's a whole
screen of text messages. Now that the international feast is Bren's idea, no one is complaining.
Instead they're offering to help. I'm not sure Dad
will have a family recipe for me, but I have an
idea.

"We're up. You ready?" Tate must have super
soft-soled sneakers, because I never hear his footsteps.

"Yeah, just one favor?" I ask with my best plead-
ing voice.

"Anything."

Oh boy, now, that's an answer.

"Pay no attention to the girl in the cell phone,"
I say. I hit FaceTime on Mayleen's contact page,
and within seconds her bright, cheery face is up
on my screen.

"Hey, Kenzie," she says with a wave. "Aren't you
going to introduce me to your friend?"

Tate squeezes into the camera's view and waves
back.

"This is Scarecrow," I say.

"That is definitely not the Scarecrow I remember." She giggles, and Tate takes the compliment with his usual charm.

When we get up the stairs, I casually set the phone up at the edge of the stage and whisper. "Now be quiet. The show's about to start."

As the music for "We're Off to See the Wizard" begins, Mayleen makes reindeer antlers with her thumbs stuck in her ears and sticks out her tongue. Her antics continue through the whole song.

And while I might be laughing at inappropriate places, at least I'm onstage, singing, and experiencing what it's like to just be a girl in middle school.

chapter twelve

can't believe how well this came together," I say to Bren. Book club is in the caf today since food isn't allowed in the library.

"Not bad, sunshine," he says. "Maybe you should consider taking on a bigger role in the club."

I plop some pad thai onto the last free spot on my plate and head toward a table. Bren and I sit down.

"I've already bitten off more than I can chew," I say, the irony of taking a big bite of a quesadilla not escaping me.

Bren laughs. "I'd say so."

When I can speak without food in my mouth, I clarify. "I mean I'm already running for student council and doing the musical," I say. "Plus, Ashia and I are planning to go ice-skating, and I'm taking photography lessons and hoping I can join the photography club."

Bren stares at me. "Geez. It's like you were raised by wolves and you've never seen a middle school before." He laughs again.

Yeah, well, maybe not wolves, but do hotel employees and flight attendants count?

"This stuff wasn't available at my old school." I finally decide on the right words. "And I'm excited. But I'm realizing I can't do it all."

Divi, who writes for the school's digital newspaper, sits next to me. She's been really helpful in spreading the word about our campaign. "Hi, Kenzie. Ashia asked me to remind you you're supposed to help with her speech after this."

There's all this delicious-smelling food in front of me, and I can't seem to find a moment to eat it. I try for a quick response. "I know. She already reminded me this morning, at lunch, and at the end of the day." As if Ashia has a secret camera on us, at that moment a text message from her comes through— reminding me to come to her house after book club.

"Thanks again for helping with the campaign,"

I say. "And with the feast. Which food is yours?"

She points to the bread on my plate. "It's called naan. My mom makes it every night with dinner, so it was super easy to bring in."

I use the conversation as an opportunity to eat. The bread is warm, and I love how the crunchy brown bubbles go perfectly with the soft parts of the bread. "Yum," I say. Forget not talking with your mouth full. This stuff is worth it.

"You should come over some time," says Divi. "If you think this is good, wait until you taste the rest of a Patil family meal."

"I'd really love that. Let's do it soon," I say. Because that is something I do not want to miss, and my window of opportunity is getting smaller and smaller.

"Which one is yours?" asks Divi as Bren looks on.

I point to the fondue pot. "My ancestors came from all over the place," I say. "I picked a Swiss cheese fondue."

"Good call," says Bren, clearing the last bit of food on his plate. "I'm ready for round two." He's up and at the food table with lightning speed.

"Thanks for putting all this together," says Divi. "We're glad you're here. I hope you're liking your new home." She gets up and heads over to the fon-due pot, where Bren is still piling bread and vege-tables on his plate.

My new home.

I take a deep breath and close my eyes, sud-denly feeling like Dorothy in the middle of Oz.

It's Friday, aka Debate Day. I've practiced Ashia's speech with her the last couple days, and she's totally ready for it. I head to the auditorium to meet up and listen to her go over it one more time.

But instead of Ashia, Divi is waiting at the stage door for me.

"I'm so glad I found you, Kenzie," she says. "I have some bad news."

Uh-oh. That is never a good start to a conversa-tion. "What's wrong?" I ask.

"Ashia went home sick," she says. "She asked me to let you know. She is so disappointed to be missing this, but the nurse wouldn't let her stay with the throwing up and all."

"Well, that explains why she wasn't eating at lunch," I say. "But who's going to debate?"

Divi just stares at me, like she's afraid to say what she needs to say.

"No way, Divi. Public speaking and I do not go well together," I say, walking away from her.

She grabs my arm and I have no choice but to stand there and listen. "She needs you, Kenzie. You know her speech and all her debating points. And technically, this is your job: to back up the future class president."

"Divi, I can't. I mean, I physically cannot get up there and debate," I say. "The thought of everyone staring at me makes me all shaky. I can't even look at all those kids out there."

"So don't look at them," she says. "Problem solved, right?"

"No, problem is not solved," I insist. "I can't go up there and talk in front of the entire seventh-grade class."

Bren appears out of nowhere and exchanges looks with Divi.

"You can do this, Kenzie," he says. He guides me backstage and pulls out a chair so I can sit down. "Rule number one: Make eye contact with one person at a time. It will help you focus. Rule number two: If you need time, pause for ten seconds. Everyone will think you did it to make a statement, and you'll have their complete attention."

I can tell Divi is as impressed as I am. "How do you know all this?" I ask.

"I listen to TED talks," he says.

"You're kidding! I thought I was the only kid who did that," I say. I'm about to say that my dad regularly assigns them as homework, but stop myself from giving too much of that life away.

"Hold the phone," says Divi. "Who the heck is Ted and why are you two being so gushy about him?"

Bren and I laugh. "They're short, really powerful talks from people all over the world," I say.

"Well, okay," says Divi. "Sounds like you've studied enough of them to know how to do it, then, yes?"

I take a deep breath. I guess maybe I have. "You're right. If we want a shot to win this thing, I have to do this."

A few minutes before the debate, my mind is totally ready. My body, however, has not gotten the message. I'm still shaky. My knees are more like marshmallows than bones. My heart thinks it's the front-runner in an Ironman race.

The sounds of auditorium seats being folded down and students chatting with their friends fill my ears. "Why do I keep doing this?" I say to Divi.

"Doing what?" she asks. "You keep running for class council?"

"No. I keep putting myself in situations where I'm on that stage, with all those eyes watching me," I say. "Why?"

Divi sits down next to me. "Because this is your chance," she says. "To see what you can do."

For a second I wonder if she knows my secret.

"Kenzie, you're smart and you're brave," says Divi. "You've got this."

You're brave. It's probably not a good thing to start crying before a big debate, but Divi's words are exactly what I need right now. I give her an enormous hug, so tight that she coughs when I squeeze her.

"Sorry," I say as I let go. "But you are seriously the best."

Mr. Kumar pokes his head around the corner. "Kenzie, it's time." And just like that, he's gone.

"I'll stay backstage," promises Divi. "Turn to your right and I'll be here cheering you on."

I nod and make my way to the front, but there's one more thing I need to do.

I tap my phone screen, and Mayleen's face fills it up in no time. "I won't say a word," she says. "Good luck."

"Thanks," I whisper. Divi's words and Mayleen's smile will get me through this.

I set the phone on the podium in front of me and adjust my notes. Only then do I turn to Tate and do my best to smile like I'm not one teensy bit nervous. He reaches out and we shake hands, but he holds on a couple of seconds more at the end than standard hand-shaking procedure would require.

"Welcome to the official debate for seventh-grade class president," says Mr. Kumar. "Due to circumstances beyond our control, vice presidential candidate Kenzie Rhines will be filling in for presidential candidate Ashia Boyce. I will ask a question proposed by the seventh grade, and each candidate will be given time to answer. At the end, they will make their closing statements. Please be considerate of your fellow classmates as you listen to their responses." He looks directly at a few of the biggest troublemakers before addressing the class again. "Now, ladies and gentleman, please give a big hand to your student council hopefuls, Kenzie Rhines and Tate O'Dea."

The audience erupts and I instantly have a flashback to elementary school. Whenever there was anything at all that gave us a chance to be loud, we were. Middle school is apparently no different. Mr. Kumar quiets the crowd with a wave of his hand.

"Question number one," he says. "What qualities do you and your vice president possess that would make you the best choice? We'll start with Miss Rhines."

We prepared this one, but as I think back to my backstage pep talk with Divi, a new answer comes to mind. "Thank you, Mr. Kumar. And thank you all for taking the time to listen to what we have to say." The first thing you always do is thank the moderator and the people—that much I know. You mess that one up and you're already toast.

"A good friend just informed me that I'm smart and I'm brave, although I'm not sure I would have ever described myself that way. But I do thank her for her kind words."

I try to make eye contact with one person in the

audience like Bren said, but when I do, it hits me that the entire seventh-grade class is out there. More than two hundred kids. All eyes on me. Darn it, now I have sweaty palms, too. I focus on my notes but catch Mayleen waving her hands frantically, which manages to get my attention. She takes a deep breath herself and motions with her hands for me to do the same. I do.

"I'm organized," I say. "My dad and I travel quite a bit, and I'm the one who keeps all the schedules, flight information, and info on the best tourist spots handy. I'm also the one who remembers to bring extra pretzels, because you never want pretzels as much as you do on an airplane once that little bag is empty, right?"

The audience laughs, giving me a small shot of confidence.

"I'm a good student, I'm willing to take on challenges, and I believe that everyone's voice should be heard." As the words come out of my mouth, I understand more about myself than I even thought I did. "I'm a team player, and most of all I'm . . ."

No, Kenzie. Do not do this again.

But it's not stage fright that stops me from

speaking this time—it's the lie that I'm trying to force out. That I'm dependable.

In one sense, I am. I've always been the one who people can count on. If I say I'll do something, I'll do it. But now, standing in front of all these people who believe that if they vote for me I'll be their dependable vice president, I'm not so sure I am. What dependable person runs for class council when she knows she won't even be here to do the job?

Mayleen is waving her arms again on my phone screen. When she has my attention, she mouths the perfect words.

I take a ten-second pause.

"I'm sorry," I say. "Sometimes my brain runs ahead of me a bit. What I meant to say was that, most of all, I'm so very happy to be here, and I would love to be your choice for seventh-grade vice president."

Mayleen gives me a thumbs-up and a big smile as the crowd once again takes the chance to get loud.

I launch into what was supposed to be Ashia's speech, giving the audience all the reasons why they should vote for her. Because she's the reason

I'm up here doing this, and I am not going to lose this for her.

"You will not find a more qualified candidate than Ashia Boyce," I say. And against my better judgment, I turn to my opponent.

Okay, Tate, bring it on.

chapter thirteen

Maybe this wasn't such a good idea.

I'm hanging on to the boards at the ice rink like I've completely forgotten how to skate.

"Need a little help?" Tate skates backward in front of me as I push my way forward.

"I'm fine," I say. "It's just been a while." I let go and force myself to skate away from the boards.

He holds out his gloved hand. "Come on. You may have kicked my butt at the debate yesterday, but I won't hold that against you."

Oh man, that smile.

Ashia, luckily feeling much better, is across the ice with Divi, and they're waving their arms in a *take his hand and skate* kind of way. Well, okay then.

I grab Tate's hand and let my feet glide as his momentum takes us around the ice. I'm not fully aware of what this must look like until a group of kids from school stop mid-ice and stare.

"Don't worry," he says, squeezing my hand tighter. "They'll all gossip no matter what we do. Let's skate."

As we go by the benches, Divi shouts, "Great event, Kenzie!"

This Saturday skating adventure is part of our campaign strategy—showing our class that under our leadership there will be some great events and chances for us all to get together outside of school. Of course, it's a total bonus for me, because I get to go hang out with everyone, and I have to say, it's pretty amazing. And since Dad is miraculously not working this weekend, it made sense to do it now. I was so pumped at the end of the debate that I invited everyone along. Seemed like a great time to announce it. I guess I shouldn't have been surprised when they showed up.

A bunch of kids skate up next to us when we get to the other side. "Thanks for the invite, Kenzie," says a boy from my science class. "We should do this stuff more often."

The girl next to him is skating like it's as simple as walking. "Yeah, you and Ashia are going to make a great team," she says. "Sorry, Tate."

"Sure," I say. "And thanks." The group skates off, and I ease up on Tate's hand. "Sorry," I say. "No one knows who's going to win."

Tate skates backward, taking both of my hands and guiding me along the ice. "You're going to win, Kenzie," he says. "I fought the good fight, but people love you guys. My goodness, even Shelby helped with your campaign."

"Yeah, I'm pretty sure Shelby will be voting for you." I laugh, and a look of realization comes over Tate's face.

"Oh" is all he says. "Well, all I can say is that even I'm voting for you."

I'm sorry—what now?

"You're supposed to vote for yourself," I say. "It's tradition."

"No more election talk." Tate spins to the side of me, but I let go of his hand and wave as I skate past him. It's nothing that will earn me an Olympic medal, but I am standing on my own two feet.

* * *

Tuesday morning. Election Day.

Apparently, it's quick and painless. Everyone votes in homeroom and the winners are announced at the end of the day. I'm not sure why I'm so nervous. I mean, either way, Dad and I are leaving in less than three weeks.

So why do I want this so bad? Is it really just for Ashia?

Ashia catches me in the hall. "Kenzie! This is going to be great. We'll be able to do so much and make so many changes around here for the better."

I put my hands on her shoulders. "Ashia, take a breath."

She does. "I'm so excited."

"Yes, I can see that," I say, heading in the direction of homeroom. "I am too, but this could go either way."

This time, she stops me. "Girl, you have this whole place into this election," she says. "You're planning skating parties, international feasts, and apparently some photography contest?"

"Oh yeah, did I not tell you about that?" I say innocently. "This town is so beautiful and there are so many talented kids in this school, I thought it would be fun. My dad's friend is a big-time photographer and he offered to judge."

"See, this is what I'm talking about," she says. "Things have changed ever since you arrived."

Since I arrived. How much will things change when I leave?

The warning bell for homeroom goes off.

"Good luck," says Ashia. "Don't forget to vote for yourself!" And she's off as the massive crowds filter into classrooms like swarms of bees.

This is exactly what I wanted. The chance to see what I can do, on my own, with no one around me who *has* to give me what I want. So why is the tiny cloud of guilt I've been carrying turning into a raging tornado inside me right now?

See, there's what I'm *supposed* to do as a candidate and what I probably *should* do, and the two of them are having an all-out tug of war. I want this for Ashia, I really, really do, but if we win, it won't be fair to anyone. Tate and his running mate are a real going-to-be-here-to-do-the-job team, but Ashia will only be half a team. I let the two sides tug and tug and tug until I'm sure of what I need to do.

When the teacher passes out the ballots, I skip over my name and check the box for Tate O'Dea and his running mate.

At the end of the day, Mr. Kumar's voice comes on over the loudspeaker. "Good afternoon, boys and girls, this is your principal with an exciting announcement."

He says it's exciting, but there is never any change in the tone of his voice, so I'm not sure if I should believe him.

"We have the results of the sixth-, seventh-, and eighth-grade elections," he continues.

As always, the kids take the chance to hoot and holler until they're told to stop.

"I'm happy to hear your enthusiasm," Mr. Kumar says. "Now let's all be great listeners as I read the results."

He goes through the sixth-grade winners, and the echoes of cheers make their way through the halls.

"And now for the seventh-grade results."

Here it is.

But as he lets the sixth-grade cheers get quieter, Ashia and Bren are coming through the doorway of my math class. They both rush over, giving the teacher a wave (he responds with a knowing nod), and they crouch next to my chair on either side.

"We couldn't stand not being here with you," says Ashia. "So we got special permission." I wrap an arm around her for a half hug and give Bren a smile.

As Mr. Kumar announces the secretary and treasurer, I weave my fingers together and squeeze hard. Ashia is bouncing on her toes, and Bren is gripping the metal bar of my chair. Wow. I didn't realize how big a deal this is for people. My guilt tornado is now out of control, but my nerves have taken over, and my heart—the part that still wants this despite everything—is telling the rest of me to SHUSH.

"Our new vice president and president of the seventh-grade class council are . . ."

Ashia grabs my hand.

chapter fourteen

W ell, this is a first," says Mr. Kumar. And he stops. The entire school is silent, waiting for the winner of the seventh-grade president position.

"What's a first?!" Ashia shouts out, getting a laugh from the class.

"Sorry for the delay, folks," says the principal. "It appears we have our first-ever tie."

A chorus of "huh" and "what" surrounds me.

"Looks like we'll have seventh grade co-presidents and co–vice presidents this year. Congratulations to Ashia Boyce and Kenzie Rhines *and* Tate O'Dea and Paul Vangen." He goes on to announce the eighth-grade winners, but I don't pay attention to any of it. I just sit here.

"Kenzie," says Ashia, shaking my shoulder. "We won! Well, sort of, but we still won. Are you okay?"

We won. Sort of. I'm seventh-grade co–vice president.

Someone grabs my hand and gives it a squeeze, but it's not from Ashia's side. "Hey, Kenzie," whispers Bren. "This is awesome. Get out of your head."

I don't know why it's Bren's voice that brings me back to reality, but I'm thankful for it. I shake out my arms and get to my feet.

"Thank you. Thank you. Thanks so much. We'll do our best." I try to get to everyone who's congratulating us, but before long the bell to go home rings, and everyone but me, Ashia, and Bren is gone. Even the teacher has left for bus duty.

"Soooo," says Ashia. "Are you okay with this?"

My first thought is *YES, I'M OKAY WITH THIS!* Not only do I get to be on student council with Ashia and Tate (okay, yeah, so it's only for a couple weeks), but when I leave, I don't even need to find a replacement because there's already a vice president.

But my second thought is that I will eventually have to tell everyone—EVERYONE—that I'm leaving and I knew it all along.

"Yeah, no, this is great," I say. Not a chance I'm telling her I voted for Tate and we would have won if I hadn't. "In a way, this is even better, isn't it? I mean, it's Tate." And that's when Bren's face goes all weird.

"I gotta go," says Bren, slinging his backpack over his shoulder. "Congratulations, Kenzie."

I grab for his arm. "Wait, are you mad?"

He gives me a look I can't read. "No, I'm not mad. Enjoy your victory." He leaves. Just like that. And I have no clue what's going on with him.

"Why is he upset?" I ask Ashia. We pack up our things and head for the hallway.

"Are you seriously that clueless?" she asks.

"I have no idea what you're talking about," I say. And I really don't.

"He's not mad, Kenzie. He's jealous."

We say a few thank-yous to students congratulating us as we walk by. "Then why didn't he run for office?" I ask.

"Not of you winning, silly. Of Tate."

"Bren's jealous that Tate won?" I am totally lost.

Ashia stops. "Kenzie, if you can't figure this out on your own, I'm not going to be the one to tell you." She waves as she heads for the front doors, leaving me with a swarm of new congratulators.

"Tell me what?!" I yell after her. But my only source of information on this mystery is long gone.

It's the leads at musical rehearsal today, which means I run into Tate as soon as I get there.

"My partner in crime," he says, walking up the aisle toward me. "What do you think about the tie?"

"Crazy, right?" I say.

"And to think if I hadn't voted for you, we would have won," he says.

Part of my brain says to keep my mouth shut, but the other part that doesn't always think things through spits out the words. "Well, turns out if I hadn't voted for *you*, we would have won."

Tate stops before we get to the front row. "Hold on a second. You voted for me?"

I bite my lip, but can't manage to hold back the smile fighting its way out. "Yes, but don't you dare tell Ashia."

He pretends to zip his lips and smiles. "We're going to make quite a team, Vice President Rhines," he says, dropping his bag on one of the seats.

"Co–Vice President Rhines," I correct.

"Right. Hey, since there's no school on Friday, do you want to meet up at my house to work on some ideas and plans?" he asks. "Plus, we should probably be rehearsing lines."

My mind races back to the first day of school (*my* first day of school), when Tate O'Dea whipped by in a blur. And now he's asking me to come over his house? Not even a top concierge like Fiona could have arranged this. THIS is all me.

"Yeah, sure. Sounds good," I say. "Wait, why is there no school?"

"Nevada Day," says Tate. "A little-known bonus of living here."

I smile. And even though I certainly don't need a day off already, I don't mind one bit that I'll get to spend part of it with Tate. Rehearsal goes by without any trouble, meaning they still haven't made me practice my solo, and I'm doing okay (even without Mayleen making faces in my phone) singing the group numbers and rehearsing lines.

But when Mrs. Summers sits us down to go over the schedule for the next month, there's a bit of a problem.

"As you know, we have off on Friday and then there are staff development days Monday and Tuesday," she says. "So I'd like to start practices on Saturdays in order to be ready for the performance, and I'll need all of you to be here. Are there any conflicts?"

Any conflicts? Um, yeah.

The boy playing the Cowardly Lion speaks up. "I have soccer, but the games are in the afternoon."

"We were thinking ten a.m. to twelve would be best," says Mrs. Summers. "Does that work?"

Lion nods.

Everyone else seems to be fine with it, and this is my chance to say something. But if I do, it's all over. *Over.* And I'm not ready for that.

"My dad usually travels on the weekends for work and I go with him," I say. "I don't think I can do Saturdays."

Mrs. Summers taps her pencil on her clipboard. "Every weekend?" she asks.

"Almost," I answer. "Shelby could fill in for me. She's the understudy and she really hasn't gotten much stage time."

Mrs. Summers looks to the ceiling and touches

her pencil to her chin. "It's not ideal, Kenzie, but if you can't be here, you can't be here. Will it be a problem for the performance?"

Until now, I've been able to fudge my answers, but that one is a pretty direct question.

I can tell her I'll be here, but that's not the truth.

I can tell her I won't be here, but then I'll lose everything.

"Kenzie, honey, are you okay?" asks Mrs. Summers. The Cowardly Lion, the Scarecrow, and the Tin Man (who is actually a tin girl) are all staring at me.

Or I can tell her a half-truth.

"By then my dad won't have to leave here every weekend," I say. My blood is pumping as I wait for her response.

"Great. I'll tell Shelby we need her to take over for you on Saturdays," she says. "But do try to be here if you can."

I nod.

We all pack up our things and head up the aisle toward the doorway. When the others get up ahead of us, Tate leans over and whispers, "If I didn't know better, I'd say you were hiding something, Kenzie

Rhines." And without even looking back at me, he steps ahead and disappears to the left.

"Except you're right," I say out loud. But there's nobody there to catch my words.

chapter fifteen

've done what I set out to do. I got the lead in the musical. I'm on the seventh-grade student council. I run book club events. I'm decent again at ice-skating. I can even take some great pictures. *I should tell them now.*

Or maybe I shouldn't.

After the election results and musical rehearsal yesterday, I felt so guilty I told Mayleen what's been going on. Someone out of town seemed like the best option, and I didn't think telling Erin and Caitlin back in California that I've been lying to my new friends was the best way to rekindle our friendship. I text Mayleen.

You can't tell them, she writes back. You have

two and a half more weeks and then it won't matter.

But it does matter, I type. I didn't think it would, but it does.

We already went over this when I told her the truth, and we both agreed that I'd gone too far to turn back now. But what am I supposed to do, leave without saying a word?

You're in a pickle, my friend, she writes back. Sorry, gotta go. Chat later!

Ashia will be here any minute, and I don't know if I can be around her right now without cracking. Dad pops his head in my room.

"Hey, sweetie," he says. I put down my phone and give him the okay to come in. He sits down on my bed. "How's school going? We haven't had a chance to talk much since we've been here."

I'm used to Dad being gone all day, but I miss all the airport and airplane quality time we usually have. "It's all right."

"Really? Only all right?" he asks. "You've been staying after for so many activities. I thought you were having a great time."

Dad knows I'm part of the musical, but he somehow got the impression I'm helping to build sets—an easy job to leave. And he knows I helped

Ashia with her election campaign, but I might have left out that we were working on mine, too.

"Book club is going pretty well," I say. As he sits there, I wonder if I can tell him. Maybe Dad's the one who can help me figure this out.

"I'm glad," he says. "It's great they're letting you be a part of all this even knowing our circumstances."

My shoulders droop, and I play with a loose string on my sock. Maybe Dad can't help me.

"Oh, before I forget, I have two location choices for this weekend," he says.

I wait, hoping they're good ones. Getting away might be exactly what I need right now.

"Denver," he says.

Fiona. Apple pie. Yes.

"Or Minnesota." He smiles, and I know exactly why.

"The Judy Garland Museum?! Can we go?" I ask.

"I told them I could only make it if I didn't have to work on Saturday from ten to five." He reaches for my hand. "It's up to you."

This should be a tough one, but I'm sure we'll be in Denver again within a few months anyway. "Dad, they have an actual yellow brick road there."

He laughs. "Grand Rapids it is."

I leap forward and wrap my arms around him, hugging him tight. "I love you, Dad."

"I love you too, sweetie," he says.

The doorbell rings, breaking up the moment. I'd almost forgotten I'd been waiting for Ashia. It's still so strange when my two worlds collide. I'm never quite sure exactly which one is real and which one will someday be just an adventure I went on once.

I was so very much on cloud nine once Ashia got to my house yesterday that I didn't even consider telling her about my upcoming departure. We talked about this weekend's trip, the musical, the election, the next seventh-grade skating party. But not the fact that there was something I was both dying to tell her and scared to death to tell her.

At musical rehearsal after school, it's time for my big solo of "Somewhere Over the Rainbow." It's been a week and a half since my epic panic-and-run-offstage disaster, but I'm definitely much more comfortable up there after practicing group numbers and surviving the debate, and I really, really think I'm ready to give it a shot.

Mrs. Summers wastes no time diving right in. "All right, everyone. We have a lot to get through, so let's get started." She turns to me. "Are you ready, Kenzie?"

I nod about a gazillion times in only a few seconds.

I make my way up to the stage. One small step at a time.

I move the microphone switch to on.

I take a deep breath.

Not only is Ashia sitting in the front row smiling at me, but so is Tate, and so are Bren and Divi, who aren't even in the musical. I guess I shouldn't have mentioned it was solo day.

I take another deep breath, the music starts, and the words finally come out of my mouth.

I picture being with Dad on an airplane as I sing about the clouds. And I remember Mom when I sing about rainbows.

The song is all about having dreams. About chasing those dreams. About asking yourself why you shouldn't be able to chase your dreams too.

And as I finish the song as softly as Judy did, I've decided to take her advice.

chapter sixteen

After musical rehearsal, I motion Ashia backstage.

"What's going on?" she asks.

Kids are still milling around, and stage crew isn't done for the day yet. But we're tucked away behind the curtains.

"I have to tell you something." My heart is racing, and I can't form the words I want to say.

"Okay, so tell me," says Ashia.

"I haven't been completely honest with you, and I need to confess something," I say, but after the words come out, I smack myself on the forehead. "No, that's not a good start. What I mean

is, I hope you'll understand why I did what I did."
Smack. This isn't going well.

"Kenzie, just say it." Ashia puts down her things
and sits down on the floor. I follow suit and sit
next to her.

She'll understand. I tell myself. But I'm not
sure I believe it.

"You know how in the song, Dorothy wonders
why she shouldn't be able to follow her dreams
like the bluebirds?"

Ashia looks at me, clearly confused. "Yeah."

"Well, I was kind of like Dorothy when I got
here," I say. "There was so much I wanted to try,
but I knew I shouldn't, but then I thought, why
not? It's probably the only chance I'll ever get."

She waits.

"And there were some really good reasons why
not, but there were maybe even better reasons to
do it anyway." I stop, knowing full well she doesn't
have any idea what I'm talking about. "Okay,
here's the thing. You know how my dad and I go
on those business trips on the weekends?"

"Uh-huh."

"Well, that's what we usually do . . . all the time,"

I say. "He's an environmental consultant, and we travel from city to city, never staying in one place for more than a few days."

"Kenzie, I'm not sure what you're getting at," says Ashia.

There's some commotion near us as kids search for props.

I speak more quietly. "I'm only here for six weeks,"I finally spit out. And then I freeze, because I have no idea what she's going to say.

"What do you mean, six weeks?" she asks, clearly a little confused. "You're leaving?"

I nod.

"You're leaving, in what . . ."

I save her from trying to figure it out. "Two weeks."

Her eyes go wide and she takes a deep breath. "You're leaving in two weeks and you didn't think that was important information to share?"

Right now I'm wishing I hadn't picked this spot to tell her the truth. There are way too many people still around.

"I tried to. A few times," I say. "I kept telling you I wouldn't be here for the musical. I told you I wouldn't be here to be vice president. But you kept saying I was making excuses."

"You could have corrected me, Kenzie," she says.

"I tried. I really did. But you don't understand how much I needed this," I say. "And I have it all figured out. When I leave, there's already another vice president to fill in for me, and Shelby will take over Dorothy's role. Nobody will even care."

Her eyes turn to thin slits as she takes another deep breath and stands up. "I'll care," she says. She picks up her bag and takes off without another word.

Just when I think it couldn't possibly get any worse, someone comes through the curtains. And when she smiles her devious smile, I'm certain she's heard enough to totally take me down.

Shelby.

chapter seventeen

'␣ve been going crazy all morning. Ashia isn't
returning my texts, and Shelby hasn't tried to
contact me after our run-in yesterday. I should
be excited for our trip to Minnesota, but school
is closed for Nevada Day and I have to wait for
what seems like forever for Dad to be done with
work.

My new chaperone is here, but she's much
more interested in doing her college homework
than paying any attention to me. Hey, Nannies to
Go—"extensively screened" doesn't necessarily
mean interesting.

I try watching TV. I pick up a book and
attempt to read. I consider cleaning my room

until I stand in the doorway and remember there's really nothing in it.

If only I had some idea what was happening. Does Ashia hate me now? Does Bren know? Oh man, does Tate know? Is that why we never did set a time to get together today?

The questions keep coming, especially the big one—what will Shelby do?

Not only do I have the entire weekend to let all this stir around in my brain, but we're also off on Monday and Tuesday for staff development. Dad has never closed "school" for five days straight in all the time he's been teaching me. I guess I should be grateful I don't have to face anyone.

And just when I decide it's probably a good thing there's no school so I can avoid the impending disaster, the doorbell rings.

"Ken, you gonna get that?" the chaperone calls up the stairs.

Seriously? I clomp down the stairs to the front door, and she's sitting on the floor with her books spread all over the coffee table. "My name is Kenzie," I say.

"Yeah, I shorten everything," she says. "Funny, since I insist everyone call me Alexandria." Ah, right, that's her name.

When I open the door, Bren is standing there, hands in his pockets.

"Hi," I say, the surprise making its way into my voice.

"Hey. You busy?" he asks.

From the other room, Alexandria decides to peep up. "Is that a boy? You can't have a boy in the house, K."

Bren lowers his eyebrows.

"Chaperone," I say. "Apparently Ken wasn't a short enough nickname for me."

I slink through the front door. "No problem, Alex," I call into the house. "We'll sit on the porch."

As I sit down, I can't stop wondering if Bren knows. But of course he does. Why else would he be here?

Brave and bold, Kenzie. Might as well ask.

"So I'm guessing you heard?" I turn away slightly.

"Heard what?" he asks. "That you and Shelby are friends now?" His face has a questioning sort of look.

"Definitely not," I say. "Why would you ask that?"

"I ran into her on my way over here and she said to tell you she said hi," he answers.

She's clearly up to no good, but there's something more important I have to ask. "So wait, why are you here?"

"I wanted to drop this off." He hands me a picture book on onomatopoeias. "My sister got it at her school book fair, and I thought you'd like it."

I smile, remembering the day I discovered Brent is a poetry nerd just like I am. "That's really sweet. Thank you. I'll return it to you next week, if that's okay."

As if on cue, ruining the moment, my phone buzzes with a text from Shelby.

Give up Dorothy. Or everyone will know who you really are.

I'm not quick enough hiding it from Bren and he reads over my shoulder.

"I'm assuming Dorothy means the *role* of Dorothy and not some doll or dog or something?"

I nod.

"And I'm guessing you have a pretty big secret you don't want to get out," he says.

I nod again.

"You do realize you're being blackmailed, right?" he asks.

Nod.

We sit in silence for a few minutes before Alexandria pops her head out. "You guys okay out here?" she asks.

"Yes" is all I answer. Although I am so *not* okay.

Once she's inside, I turn so I'm facing Bren. "Aren't you going to ask what it is?"

"What what is?" he asks.

"The secret," I answer. "The thing Shelby is using to blackmail me."

"Nope."

Wow. Ashia won't talk to me, and Shelby is totally taking advantage, but not Bren. I don't get this kid.

"You probably won't want to be my friend anymore once you find out," I say.

Bren sits back and fakes a shocked expression. "Whoa. Hold on. Are you saying we're friends, sunshine?"

I let out a little laugh. "I'm saying not for long."

He leans forward, arms on his knees, and focuses on his sneakers. "Listen, I have a lot of friends, but nobody quite like you," he says with a smile. "I don't plan on giving that up anytime soon."

I smile back, wondering how I missed this side of him.

"Also, you've taken over so many of my book club duties that I have time to play video games after school now," he says. "So that alone is worth keeping you around."

I bump my shoulder into him, letting him know I don't appreciate the joke.

"You shouldn't let Shelby boss you around," he says.

"If I don't, she'll tell," I say.

"Would that be so bad?" he asks.

I want to tell him he doesn't know. I want to give him the whole story and explain. But I also don't want him to run away screaming.

"You should scoop her," he says. "Put the truth out there yourself."

I'm about to let him know exactly how crazy he is, until I get an idea. "You might actually be onto something."

He waits as I plop my face into my hands and rub my forehead for a minute.

"Will you help me?" I ask.

"Yeah, of course."

"Great. We need to call Divi." I grab his hand and pull him into the house, past Alexandria the chaperone, who is too busy with her nose in a book to notice. When we get to the kitchen, I pick up my phone and find Divi's number.

I text Divi three times and leave her two messages. I finally get one back.

What's the emergency?

I call her immediately. Bren's right: The old-fashioned pick-up-the-phone-and-call method is so much easier than texting for half an hour.

"I need your help," I say. "If you're willing."

I explain my plan to write an unofficial letter to the cast of the musical and the student council with my complete confession. But Divi is more curious about what's going on than Bren.

"I don't understand," she says. "What did you do?"

I need to tell her, especially if she's going to help me write this up, but Bren is sitting right here, and I can't bear to lose two friends at once.

"Can I write the letter and send it to you?" I ask. "I want to get the words right."

She agrees to help me and I give her a huge thank you. When I hang up the phone, Bren is heading toward the front door.

"You're leaving?" I ask. He doesn't yet realize how ironic it is that *I'm* asking him if *he's* leaving.

"I'm giving you some space," he says. "When you're ready, you'll share whatever it is with whoever needs to know."

Several names pop into my head, including the teachers and activity leaders who've helped me out since I've been here.

I walk him out to the porch. "Thank you, Bren," I say.

He gives me a little smile. "Things haven't been the same since you got here. In a good way," he says. "I just hope that whatever this is, it doesn't make you want to leave."

I take a deep breath and quietly let it out. Because I honestly don't know what I want right now.

I'm in the airport and I finally get a text from Tate.

Sorry. Parents had other plans for day off. Maybe tomorrow?

I'm guessing he doesn't know yet.

It's okay, I write back. But I'll be in Minnesota tomorrow.

Minnesota?!

Long story. Would be going to see the real ruby slippers if they hadn't been stolen.

Have fun.

Thanks. Gotta go.

I turn off my phone and lean my head on Dad's shoulder.

"Everything okay?" he asks.

"It will be," I say. "Someday, I think it will be."

Dad puts an arm around me and squeezes my shoulder. "Is it a boy?"

"No. Yes. It's a bunch of things," I say.

"But you're still liking school?" he asks.

"Yeah—I mean, I love it. It's just that middle school is a lot harder than I ever imagined it would be."

An announcement for a gate change booms over the loudspeaker, so we both stop and listen, but it's not for us.

"I'm guessing you're not talking about the schoolwork," says Dad.

"No. My teachers are much nicer than my last one." I sit up and smirk at Dad, and he smiles back at me. "Dad, did you ever keep a secret you were pretty sure you shouldn't have?"

Dad looks up at the ceiling and then at me. "Honey, we've all done that. Anything I can help with?"

I shake my head.

"How about this," he says. "You have a birthday coming up, and we can either go somewhere or have a party here next weekend and invite your new friends."

But I can't tell Dad I might not have any new friends by then. When I don't say anything, he keeps talking.

"I'm surprised you haven't brought up your birthday yet," he says. "You've usually requested a trip or some big event by now."

He's totally right. Last year we went swimming with dolphins in Florida and I had it planned for months. "I know, but not this year, Dad," I say. "I've been so busy at school and you've been really into this project, so I figured we could do something after we leave here." I pause. "Maybe go visit some friends back home?"

The word "home" sounds strange as it leaves my mouth. I'm not even sure where that is anymore.

"Do you ever think about your old school?" he asks.

I nod. "I've been meaning to call Erin and Caitlin. I still miss them."

Dad looks sad all of a sudden. "I'm really sorry you had to leave all that behind."

We have a lot of mini conversations about this stuff, but they always seem to stop before we get any deeper. This time, I decide to keep going. "I know, Dad. But the other thing we got to leave behind was the sadness. Everything there reminded me of Mom. Everything."

Dad grabs my hand as another announcement blares through the terminal. "Some days I think that's a good thing, and other days I wonder if I took you away from the only place you could have really healed."

I've wondered that too.

"But what I didn't understand then was that I didn't have to be where Mom was to be reminded of her," I say. "I think about her all the time. No matter where we go."

"Me too," he says, looking right at me. "And you're right. There are beautiful reminders of her everywhere."

"It doesn't matter if we're in the middle of South Dakota—she's there," I say. "And I'm really, really thankful for that."

Dad takes a deep breath, letting it out as he shuts his eyes. I know that move. When you miss someone more than anything, you have to shut out the real world for just a few moments, or there's no way on earth to stop the tears from falling.

I squeeze Dad's hand and take my own deep breath.

The guy at the desk makes an announcement calling for preboarders. That's us. Back to the real world, or at least our world of VIP privileges.

"How'd I get such a wonderful daughter?" asks Dad.

And while I'm grateful for his faith in me, I wonder what he'll think about his wonderful daughter lying to all her friends.

"It comes from having a wonderful dad."

We get in line without another word, but the smile on Dad's face says it all.

chapter eighteen

Saturday morning, while Dad is at work, I write my confession/apology letter to the musical cast and seventh-grade student council of Sagebrush Middle. Then I write it again. And again. But I can't get it right. How do I tell them I knew all along that I couldn't finish what I started? With every single sentence, it finally hits me how wrong what I did was.

I knew I was leaving and I did it all anyway. I justified everything, but it wasn't fair to anyone else. Maybe I should take Shelby's offer and slink away quietly.

I start my fourth rewrite but get interrupted by a text from Ashia.

Been thinking about this. You need to make things right.

I know, I text back. Working on it now.

When she doesn't write anything else, I take another turn. What was the worst part about what I did?

I expect her to say that I lied or that I'm going to let everyone down, but she surprises me.

That you didn't care what you were leaving behind.

And with that, I know what I need to write.

Dear Classmates,

After you read this letter, you will probably think very differently of me. You might wonder if you ever really knew me. And I want to say first that I do very much care about how you feel.

When I came to Sagebrush, I hadn't been to school in three years. My last school was not an ordinary school. My dad and I flew around the country for his job, and he taught me while we were in the air, or in the terminals, or sometimes in hotel lobbies. My life is very different, and I felt different, and I wanted to know what it was like to be a regular kid in a regular middle school.

The truth is, we're only here for six weeks. That's it. I leave in two weeks and I won't ever be back.

At first, I thought that was a good thing—I could try all these wonderful middle-school things that I'd normally be too scared to do, and then leave and never look back if it didn't work out. Because we're always on the road, I never have to think of anything long-term. And when I'm on the road, it's always VIP: first class, fancy hotel rooms, backstage passes, celebrity dinners. I know, it probably sounds like I shouldn't be complaining, and I'm not, really, but even with all that, I don't have the things you do. And, as it turns out, I really love those things.

I wanted to see what I could do as a
"normal" middle schooler, and I had
a plan—at least I thought I did. It
wasn't such a good one.

So I accepted the lead role in the
musical. And I took on co-vice
president. And I never said a word.
And for that I'm truly sorry.

But most of all, I'm sorry I acted
like I didn't care what I was leaving
behind. I had no idea what I was
leaving behind . . . until I got to know
all of you. Until you welcomed me
and voted for me and came to watch
me sing.

I thought I deserved this chance,
because I didn't know if I'd ever
have it again. But now I see that you
didn't deserve this, and I hope that
someday you'll forgive that girl who
once upon a time went to school with
you for six weeks. Maybe that's all

I'll ever be in your memories, and
if that's the case, that's okay. But
sometimes we need to seek out the
good memories, and maybe you have
a few of those of me too.

It's all I can hope for.

Sincerely,

Kenzie Rhines

The easy thing to do would be to give in to
Shelby and let her win. After all, I'd only have
the role of Dorothy for two more weeks before I'd
have to give it up anyway. But I'm going to listen
to Ashia instead. I need to make this right.

I attach the letter to an e-mail addressed to Divi.
I ask her again to get it out for me, since she has
a student e-mail list from her school newspaper
duties. I hit send before I can even read it over. A
wave of panic washes over me, followed by relief.
Because I do care that I'll never see these people
again. But at least I'll leave with my head held high.

∗ ∗ ∗

I'm literally standing on the yellow brick road (okay, so it's in the museum, not in Oz, but still) when I get the text from Divi.

So sorry, Kenzie. Our scoop got scooped.

Huh? I text back.

Shelby let it slip at a birthday party. News spreads fast.

Oh no. It won't be long before everyone knows. Everyone.

For what it's worth, she texts, I understand.

All I can think to say is Thank you.

"Everything okay?" asks Dad, finally stopping twenty feet ahead of me.

I stare at my phone. "Um, yeah. But I have to return this message." Without waiting for a response, I run to the restroom and sit inside one of the stalls, lid down. Still gross, I know, but it's the least of my worries right now.

She told, I text Bren.

And within seconds I get a message back. I know.

I take a deep breath and let my head and shoulders drop. But when my phone rings, I bolt upright. "Hello?" I answer, without even checking the caller ID.

"You doing okay, sunshine?"

"Bren, what am I going to do? Everyone will hate me," I say.

"Not everyone."

I think I get what he means, but at the same time, I feel like I don't know much of anything. "Well, Divi did say she understands."

There's silence on the other end of the line.

"Are you still there?" I ask, pretty sure I said the wrong thing.

"I'm here."

And in those two words, I hear everything I need. "Thank you," I say.

"Are you talking to me?" a voice from outside my stall asks.

"Oh no, I'm talking to someone else," I say to clarify. Except, by accident, I make it more confusing.

"The thank-you was for someone else?" asks Bren through the phone.

"No, the thank-you was for you," I say.

Except the woman outside the stall isn't getting it. "I thought you said you were talking to someone else. Do you need some help?"

"I don't need any help," I say to answer her. But now Bren is confused.

"Fine. You don't need my help. I get it," he says.

"Wait!" I shout, getting the attention of both Bren and my new bathroom friend. I swing the stall door open.

"Listen, both of you," I say. I point to the phone. "I'm talking to my friend, Bren." I point to the lady in the red shirt and dark jeans. "Bren, I'm talking to a lady in the bathroom."

The woman smiles. "Oops. Sorry for the confusion."

I head for the door. "Bren, I have to go see some *Wizard of Oz* memorabilia because I've been looking forward to this for years and I'm not going to let Shelby ruin that for me." I stop talking because I'm out of breath.

"O-kay," says Bren. "Call me later?"

I nod like he can hear me. "Oh, right, I will." I hang up the phone and put it in my pocket. I turn to apologize to the lady in the bathroom, but she's already in one of the stalls.

Dad is waiting for me when I get out to the hallway. "Now is everything okay?" he asks. "There's obviously something you're not telling me."

I want to tell him. I really do. But he'll be so disappointed in me, and I can't take any more of that right now.

"For now, Dad, can we say I have a few things to fix and leave it at that?" I ask.

Dad puts an arm around me. "Sure. Let's be off to see the Wizard."

And as if nothing in the world is wrong, we skip down the yellow brick road.

chapter nineteen

nstead of heading back to Las Vegas on Sunday,
Dad surprises me with another trip to DC. "Since
you have two days off from school, we're taking
a little detour."

When we get to Kuan-yin's house, I run up
the steps to the front door. Mayleen opens it and
practically tackle-hugs me on the porch.

"I am so excited to see you!" she shouts.

I laugh and catch my balance. "I can see that,"
I say. It's a strange thing that a month ago I
didn't have friends who were excited to see me,
or for that matter, friends who'd be mad at me if
I wasn't honest with them. But now I do.

The two of us run into the house, the echo of

our dads' voices behind us as we parade into the kitchen, where a million snacks are laid out.

"My mom got them ready before she left for work," she says. "You'll get to meet her later."

"I can't wait," I say. Because that's another thing I didn't have before—moms to hang out with.

We head up to her room, and Mayleen sits on her bed as I plop into the beanbag chair. It's white and fluffy and I could seriously sleep right here. Yup, no hotel on this trip. Mayleen's mom insisted.

"So, what's up, Kenzie?" asks Mayleen. "Your face is telling me things."

I bite my lip. I can trust her for sure, and she already knows what's been going on, but saying what I did over and over is making the guilt take hold of me.

"Everyone knows," I say. "Or they will soon."

She sits crisscross applesauce and leans forward. "Yikes. What happened?"

I tell myself not to do one of my long sentences, but I feel it coming anyway. "I told Ashia because it was getting so hard not to and I thought she'd understand, but she didn't, she really didn't. And Shelby overheard. Do you believe that? She was standing there probably the whole time and I didn't even know."

Mayleen's eyes get wide. "Uh-oh. What did she do?"

"Nothing at first, but then she texted me and said that I better give up Dorothy or she'd tell," I say, taking a breath. "But Bren convinced me to tell everyone first, and Ashia said I had to make it right, so I wrote a letter that Divi was going to send out to the cast of the musical and the student council."

"Okay, okay," says Mayleen. "That's a good idea, I think."

"Except before Divi could send it out, Shelby decided time was up."

Mayleen pushes her top teeth to her bottom teeth. "Eep."

"Right?" I say. "So I'm standing on the yellow brick road—"

"Wait, what?" she asks.

"We were at the Judy Garland Museum," I clarify. "And I got a text from Divi. And then I sent a text to Bren and he called me, but this lady in the bathroom thought I was talking to her."

Mayleen puts a hand out. "Okay, slow down.

Your point is that by now everyone must know, right?"

"Right."

"Where's that letter?" she asks.

"On my laptop, downstairs. But I also sent a copy to Divi," I answer.

Mayleen grabs her computer from her desk and sits back on the bed, motioning for me to sit next to her. "Forward the e-mail to me from your phone," she says.

I sit quietly as she reads, not sure why I'm so nervous. She already knows everything. And she's still my friend.

"This is great, Kenzie," she says. "You say you're sorry and you explain why you did it."

"But it doesn't matter," I say, leaning back onto her pink pillows. "I didn't get it out in time."

"So what?" She closes the laptop and leans back with me. "The important thing is that you send it."

I consider what she's saying, and maybe it does make sense.

"Will it even make a difference?" I ask.

"It will to the people who matter," she says. "Let me talk to Divi." She reaches for my phone.

I probably should stop her. I should tell her to forget it. I should leave it alone. But instead I listen to my new friend and let her dial Divi's number and have a ten-minute conversation about how to make this happen. By the time she hangs up, we've reworded the letter a bit. But before she sends it off to Divi, I stop her.

"Wait. I can't send it yet," I say.

"Why not?" she asks.

"Because I need to make things right with Ashia first," I say. "That apology won't mean anything if it doesn't come directly from me."

"You go back Wednesday, right?" asks Mayleen.

"Yes," I say.

"May the force be with you, my friend. You're going to need it."

chapter twenty

Wednesday morning I walk through the halls with my head down. I haven't talked to Ashia since that text on Saturday, and except for Divi, I have no idea what's going on with everyone else. I'm guessing I'm about to find out.

Shelby and a couple of her friends (I still don't know their names) stop me before I get to my locker. "Hey, Kenzie," says Shelby with a wicked-witch kind of smile.

"Hi, Shelby." I push my way to my locker, only slightly knocking her out of the way. "Nice to see you."

She laughs and steps closer. "I ran into Mrs. Summers as soon as I got here this morning.

She's looking for you." She and her two minions start walking away, but then she stops. "Although I'm pretty sure Tate won't be looking for you." She laughs as she leaves.

I try to calculate the measurements of my locker to figure out if I can climb in there and hide out for the day, but I'm afraid I might not make it with only three tiny air slats.

Once I have my things ready, I head to homeroom. I run into Ashia on the way. "Oh, hi," I say.

She smiles a tight-lipped smile.

"Can we talk? Like sneak out at lunch or something?" I ask. "Please?"

She takes a few seconds before she answers. "Not today, okay? I'm not saying no, but I'm not there yet." Before I can even come up with something to respond with, she's gone.

The warning bell rings and the halls clear out, with a few people at a time disappearing into classrooms. I stand there until there aren't any more echoes in the hall and there aren't any more people to run into. But I've forgotten something important. Mrs. Summers doesn't have a homeroom to get to.

"Kenzie, can I speak with you for a minute?" she asks, coming out of nowhere.

"Oh, I, um . . . I have to get to homeroom. Sorry," I say. I'm fully aware that my attempt to walk away isn't going to work, but I have to give it my best shot.

"I'll call your homeroom teacher," she says. "It's not a problem."

We walk to the chorus room in silence and Mrs. Summers directs me to sit down. She calls my teacher and gets the okay to keep me trapped in here with no more excuses to leave.

She sits down next to me. "I think you know why I asked you here."

Asked me here? Ha.

"Yes, ma'am." There are times in life where a "sir" or "ma'am" is your best shot at proving to someone you're a respectful kid, even if the evidence suggests otherwise.

"Can I ask you something?" She doesn't wait for an answer. "Why didn't you tell us what was going on?"

All I can think is that teachers should know it's not "can" I ask, because of course you *can*. As Dad would remind me, it's "may." But I know better than to give Mrs. Summers a grammar lesson right now. Instead I clasp my fingers together and squeeze, making sure I don't look directly at her.

"I wanted to see if I could do it," I say.

"Well, that's understandable. But maybe a better solution would have been to simply ask us for some feedback," she says. "Or, fine, try out, but then come clean."

I nod. "I thought about that. I really did," I say. "But everyone was excited and I was excited and then there was Shelby and . . ." I trail off, reminding myself that it probably doesn't matter what I say. "I'm sorry. I shouldn't have misled everyone."

When the bell for first period rings, Mrs. Summers stands up. "You need to get to class. You do understand I need to recast your part?"

Time for another "Yes, ma'am." I'm hoping she'll let me leave on that note. No further humiliation. No more explaining. But no.

"You're a very talented young lady, Kenzie. But I have to say I'm disappointed."

Kids give me all kinds of dirty looks as I walk down the hall. No one says a word to me. I get that people are mad, but is this what middle school really is? People who don't even know me give me the cold shoulder just because everyone else is doing it? It gets even worse in English.

"Come see me after class, please, Miss Rhines." Mrs. Pilchard starts her lesson before I even get to my seat.

I turn around to see if Bren is still talking to me, and, thank goodness, he gives me a smile and a thumbs-up.

I pay no attention during class, even though being in the front seat makes that feat really difficult. I count the days I have left in this place. Seven and a half.

At the end of class, Mrs. Pilchard takes a few envelopes out of her desk drawer. "I received the results from the poetry contest," she says. "We have a very poetic group of students in here. Two of you got honorable mentions, and one of you won first place overall."

There are some oohs and aahs, although it's pretty clear which kids don't care one bit.

"Congratulations for the honorable mentions." She hands one envelope to a girl on the far side of the room and one to me. "Congratulations, Miss Rhines." She's saying congratulations, but her eyes are saying *Too bad you won't be here to enjoy it.*

The last one, the first-place envelope, she hands to Bren.

I turn around and give him a big smile. "Congratulations."

"Thanks. Nice job on the honorable mention," says Bren. "Good luck with Mrs. Pilchard."

I go to her desk once everyone has left, as instructed. "You wanted to see me?" I say.

"Yes," she says. "I'm very proud of you for your accomplishment, and I can't blame you for wanting to try, but the awards ceremony is in two weeks and it appears you won't be here to attend. I do hope you'll continue writing, though."

And that's it. That's all she says before shuffling through her papers, packing up her bag, and walking out the door. Aren't teachers supposed to help students? I can't be the only middle-school kid who's ever done something wrong.

Half a day to go, but here's the problem. That includes lunch. And when you're the one kid no one wants to talk to, even I know you don't set foot in the lunchroom.

chapter twenty-one

find a spot in the library where I can sneak my food. All by myself.

I'm finally going to middle school with tons of other kids, and I'm all by myself.

"Hey." Tate's voice startles me, and I spill some of my applesauce on the table.

"Hi." I go with a one-word response since I have no idea what to say to him.

"I wanted to talk to you at lunch, but I saw you duck in here," he says.

Well, at least he wanted to talk to me. But then again, so did Mrs. Summers and Mrs. Pilchard.

I wave my hand at the empty seat.

"No thanks. This won't take long," he says.

"I heard Shelby is going to be Dorothy."

"Yeah, good news travels fast," I say, biting into my sandwich so I don't have to awkwardly look busy.

"And obviously you can't be co–vice president," he says. It's like he's waiting for confirmation from me, but I'm pretty sure it's already been confirmed. "So, no need to come to the meetings."

I finish chewing. "Right. That's what I figured."

He stands there for what feels like an hour and then finally speaks. "Do you even care about what you did, Kenzie?"

There is no correct response here. Do I stay quiet? Do I attempt to apologize? He doesn't look like he's in the mood to hear it, but I decide to try anyway.

"Yes. And I'm sorry, Tate."

He pauses for only a few seconds this time. "I'm sure you are," he says.

And with that, he turns and leaves. Not that I expected anything else.

Bren and Divi seem to have accepted my apology, although they're certainly not going out of their way to be seen with me. Tate is obviously a wee bit upset with me. And Ashia? I'm still not sure if I can get her to forgive me, and I'm terrified to try.

It doesn't take long before I get my chance. When I leave the library just before the warning bell, Ashia is at her locker. I stop myself from trying to sneak by and plant my feet right in front of her before I can change my mind. "I really need to talk to you," I say.

"Kenzie, I told you this morning that I'm not ready," she says, continuing to get her books organized.

Was it really only this morning?

"I'm sorry, Ashia. I'm so very, very sorry and I want to explain."

Ashia stops what she's doing and turns to face me. "Look, I'm angry, okay? You lied to me. You lied to all of us. You let us get attached to you, knowing you were leaving in six weeks. You took on all these big responsibilities and had no intention of ever carrying them out."

I try to get a word in quick before she tells me to get lost. "So you're saying if you knew, you never would have been my friend in the first place?"

She doesn't say anything. Maybe she's thinking about what I said?

"I'm saying that I'm hurt, Kenzie. And I'm not ready for your explanation," she says. "I don't hate you. And it's not that I never want to talk to you again. But right now, give me some room to process all this, okay?"

It's technically a question, but when she grabs her things and walks away, it's obvious she's not waiting for an answer.

Thursday morning in homeroom, as I sit there trying to stay busy and ignore the fact that no one is talking to me, there's an announcement over the loudspeaker. "Kenzie Rhines, please come to the main office. Kenzie Rhines, please come to the main office."

I get why they repeat the exact same thing they just said—because no one ever listens the first time. But today, I certainly do not need it repeated to the entire school that I'm being called down to what will obviously be the principal's office.

A chorus of "ooh" echoes through the room until the teacher puts a stop to it. "Go ahead, Kenzie," he says.

I walk down the empty hallways with only

distant voices making their way through the home-room doors. In a few minutes, these halls will fill with students and talking and yelling from one end of the school to the other. It's not like that in airports. There aren't periods of empty terminals opening up to a flood of people. Only for late-night flights, when there aren't many people there to begin with. Otherwise there is always commotion. Always people stopping right in front of you who you have to maneuver around. Always activity and chatting and cell phones and the hustle and bustle of people needing to be somewhere else.

I'd like to be somewhere else right about now.

As I enter the office, I'm pretty sure even the secretary gives me the evil eye. "Have a seat," she says. "Mr. Kumar will be with you shortly."

Five seconds later he opens his office door. "You weren't kidding," I say to the secretary. She doesn't appreciate my joke.

"Miss Rhines." Mr. Kumar stands back so I have a clear path to the chair of doom sitting in front of his desk. "Have a seat."

He sits down in what is hands down the most comfortable chair in the school—the kind you can tell is pure luxury without even sitting in it. I don't say a word.

"May I call you Kenzie?" he asks, as if he had any intention of giving me a choice. At least he got the grammar right.

I nod.

"Kenzie, it has come to my attention that your stay with us will be very short," he says. "And that, as a matter of fact, you had this information all along."

I review what he said and don't find a question in there, so I let him keep talking.

"Which wouldn't be much of a problem, except that we were not aware of this fact," he says. "And, to further complicate things, you've taken on some roles and responsibilities that require you to be here longer than your short stay would allow."

I should be paying attention to his words, his tone. But more than anything, I sit here wondering why principals can't talk so regular kids can understand them.

"Kenzie, are you listening?" he asks.

"Yes, sir. You have my undivided attention." I can sound fancy too.

"To be honest, my first thought was not why you didn't tell anyone, but why your father didn't happen to mention you would only be here six weeks."

And, at this moment, I can't believe I've never had that thought. Why didn't Dad tell them?

"Maybe he didn't think you would accept me for such a short time?" I say.

"We have to take you in," he says. "Your dad is a smart man, and I imagine he'd know that."

Now I really should be paying attention, but I can't get past what he said. Why wouldn't Dad have told them?

"I honestly don't know, sir," I say. "We haven't really talked about it."

Mr. Kumar moves some papers out of his way and leans forward on his desk. "We have some other matters to deal with here first. I understand your role of Dorothy has been reassigned."

"Yes," I say. "Mrs. Summers told me yesterday."

"And your position as co–vice president has been taken care of," he says. "Paul Vangen will take over as sole vice president."

"Heard that, too," I say. And this chair I'm

sitting in? Not the most comfortable in the school. I start to fidget.

"I'm also going to suggest that you no longer attend book club, since you won't be an official student here much longer," he says.

"Book club?" I ask. I'm not sure why that one hurts the most, but it does. There's a stabbing pain suddenly making its way through my body.

Mr. Kumar makes a tent with his fingers. I swear they must have a class at Principal School on how to act exactly the same as all the other principals. Not that I've had a principal to observe in a few years.

"And it might be a good idea to sit out the open skate this weekend."

Now I can't keep myself under control. I stand up. "Seriously? But I set that up. It's an *open* skate. Open to everyone."

He gives me a minute to sit back down and take a breath. "Well, I suppose that's true," he says. "But it would probably be best if you give your fellow students some time to digest this new information."

Like that's going to make a difference. "Is that all?" I ask, not sure I can take much more of this let's-ban-Kenzie show.

"That's it," he says. "I will, of course, need to speak to your father soon as well."

I stand up again, this time with no intention of spending one more minute in this office. "I understand," I say. Because, yeah, before he can get to him, I'm going to need to speak to my father too.

chapter twenty-two

didn't even see Dad last night. Some big thing at work has had him working super late, and, lucky me, I've had chaperone Alexandria to keep me company. (Although I still call her Alex, since she insists my name is K.) And a text is definitely not the way to ask Dad why he never told my school we wouldn't be here very long. Ha. *My* school. More like a temporary place for me to study.

And now it's Friday. Status update: My new spot for lunch is the library. Also, Ashia is still avoiding me. Bren and Divi are apparently too busy with book club (which I'm no longer allowed to go to) to talk to me. But I have to give

Bren some credit, since I've gotten a few encouraging texts from him. I haven't even seen Tate in two days—I swear he changed his route to classes to avoid me. And I have nothing to do since I've been kicked out of every activity that's been keeping me busy lately. Plus, tomorrow is my birthday, and I have no friends to invite to celebrate it with me.

The good news? I have one more week to endure this place, and then I'm gone and I never have to look back.

When I get to my house after school, the front door is open, which means Dad is home early. Great, we can finally have a chat, because there are about a million things we need to talk about. But when he pops his head out the front door and quickly shuts it, I get a weird feeling about it all.

I take my time walking up the front steps and try to peek through the small opening between the curtains in the front windows. Nothing. But there is some noise. And not Dad noise. It's twelve-year-old-girl voices.

For a minute, I wonder if it's all been a hoax. If my friends have pretended to be mad at me so they can throw me a surprise party. I remind myself that that's what people do to throw you off track. I bound over to the door and slowly turn the handle to give everyone time to hide. And then I stop. There's no surprise party here for me. What was I thinking?

I go in the house like any normal day for the last five weeks and drop my bag on the floor. Yup, nobody is hiding behind anything, and Dad is probably in his office, working from home or something. "Hello? Dad?" I say, stepping into the living room. Nothing. "Dad?"

But I was wrong. From behind the couch, the chair, and the coat rack comes "Surprise!"

I stand there, stunned. It's not Ashia or anyone from school. Not *this* school anyway. It's Erin and Caitlin from my old school in California and Mayleen all the way from Washington, DC.

"What are you guys doing here?!" I ask. Mayleen hugs me first since she's closest. I run to hug my old friends, who, even though they're here with me now, I miss more than ever.

"Your dad arranged it all," says Caitlin.

"I can't believe it. I've been meaning to call you guys," I say, as Caitlin's mom and Erin's mom suddenly pop out from behind the furniture.

"Mrs. Estes! Mrs. Kim!" I shout, running to hug them too.

I finally notice that Dad is standing behind me, recording the whole thing on his phone. "I thought you could use a nice surprise," he says. "And since I couldn't convince you to invite your friends from here to a party, I came up with a different plan."

I can't stop smiling. And the roller coaster of emotions from the past week is taking a backseat to what's happening in front of me.

"We have the whole weekend planned," says Erin. "Pedicures, shopping, movies—"

"Gossiping about boys," Mayleen interrupts.

"Hey, where's your dad?" I ask Mayleen. But I get the answer before she has time to tell me.

"Happy birthday, Kenzie!" shouts Kuan-yin. "Sorry, I had to take a phone call. Looks like I missed the surprise."

Dad elbows him. "You were in charge of pictures."

Kuan-yin holds up his camera. "Well, then I better take a million extras this weekend. That okay with you, birthday girl?"

Ten minutes ago, I thought I'd lost everything. But now I'm reminded that I've only lost something I didn't really have to begin with. In this room are my friends. The ones I'll stay friends with long after I leave this place. Maybe talking to Dad can wait a few more days. Right now, I just want to enjoy this moment.

"That's perfect," I say. I grab the girls' hands and squeeze tight.

By Sunday afternoon we are all wiped out. I'd say we've covered most of Vegas in the last two days, and I've loved every single second of it. Before Caitlin and Erin leave, we swear to each other that we'll never, ever drift apart again. I mean, really, with all the technology there is today, there's no excuse. We exchange all necessary info, and when they leave for the airport, I'm already in tears. Mayleen puts an arm around my shoulder.

"We have two hours," she says. "I want updates."

We didn't talk about school at all over the weekend. Whenever it came up, I passed it off as nothing interesting to tell, and Mayleen caught my cues not to mention the musical or the election or anything else related to this whole disaster. The dads are in the kitchen having coffee and reminiscing about college, so we head up to my room and flop on the bed.

"Tell me everything," says Mayleen.

So I do. Everything from the last update I gave her. Eating in the library. Tate's silent treatment and avoidance techniques. Ashia needing space from me.

"But you know what?" I say. "I think I'm over it."

"Over being here?" she asks.

"No, I actually really like it here. Liked it here, I guess," I answer. "And I know what I did was wrong, I do. But is it really so bad that the entire school never wants to talk to me again?"

"People might need time to get past it," says Mayleen.

"Well, they can have all the time they need," I say. "But by the time they're over it, I'll be gone. So, time to move on, right?"

Mayleen sits up and grabs a pillow to put on her lap. She leans forward. "Are you really okay with leaving things like this?"

I take a minute to think about it. *Am I?*

On one hand, I've had such a great time here. The lead in a musical. Co–vice president of the seventh-grade class. Skating-party organizer. On the other hand, none of it was real. It's like I was Judy Garland, playing a role for a short period of time. Will people remember me? I have no idea. But right now, I'm not sure it matters.

"Yes," I say. "I'm okay. Right now, I just want to go back to my old life."

"You should still send the letter," says Mayleen. "You might regret it if you don't at least apologize."

I think about what she's saying. I wanted to wait until I had the chance to apologize to Ashia in person, but since that's done, I guess it's time.

"Yeah, you're probably right," I say. I pick up my phone and send a text to Divi, asking her to send my apology letter. "Might as well start wrapping things up around here."

We're interrupted when Dad calls up the stairs. "You girls ready to go?"

We turn to each other and laugh, because it's as if Dad has been listening to our conversation.

"Yes," I call down. And then, quietly, to Mayleen I say. "We most definitely are."

chapter twenty-three

Monday morning. Five days left.

When I get to my locker, Bren sneaks up behind me and makes me jump. "Hey, sunshine," he says.

"Oh, are we still doing that?" I ask. "You're okay with being seen with me?"

Bren tilts his head. "I was pretty busy last week, but I did text you," he says. "And as I recall, it wasn't me who skipped out on lunch or ignored me in English class."

I guess I was looking at the whole thing from a different perspective, convinced he was only trying to be nice. And it's true, I did pretend to

be working on an overdue assignment. Like I've
ever had overdue assignments.

"I was trying to save you the trouble of having
to act like you weren't mad at me," I say, getting
my books in order.

"Kenzie, I'm not mad at you," he says. "I'm
really going to miss you. You're only here five
more days."

A huge wave of emotion hits me out of nowhere.
I stand there, amazed that he's counting down too.
But his is a very different kind of countdown.

"Oh" is all I can manage to spit out.

"Come to lunch today," he says. "I'm sure everyone has read your letter by now, and I think Ashia
might be ready to crack." Within seconds he's
gone. Someday, someone is going to discover secret
passageways to another world in these middle-
school hallways.

I still haven't talked to Dad, but I made him
swear he'd be home for dinner tonight. Then we'll
have the big talk. There's so much I haven't told
him.

As I head down the hall to homeroom, I catch
a rare glimpse of Tate. And while I absolutely

should run in the other direction, even if it means being late, I kind of miss bold and brave Kenzie. Besides, she has less than a week to be brave before she leaves.

I've learned enough about middle school, and middle-school boys, to know you don't actually let them know you're there until it's too late for them to pretend they don't see you. "Tate, wait up!" I shout.

"I have to get to class," he says, clearly attempting to avoid me.

"Just let me apologize. Please," I say. I'm not even sure why I care. Tate loved the attention, but as soon as things got bad, he turned on me. Although I guess I can't blame him.

"I read your letter, Kenzie, and A-plus for the effort, but it's simple," he says. "You're not who I thought you were, okay?"

I figure I'm going to have to be satisfied with that, when he drops a bomb on me.

"I liked you, Kenzie." He stands there as if I'm supposed to give some kind of response, but what could I possibly say right now? "And if you had liked *me*, you would have told me the truth."

I'm completely frozen, but as soon as he takes a

step away from me, I reach for his arm. "I'm sorry.
I did—I mean I *do* like you, but I also wanted to
know what middle school was all about," I say. "It
was the only chance I'm ever going to get."

Tate doesn't shake my hand away, but he doesn't
reach for it either. "Yeah, I bet you'll really miss
the homework from Mrs. Pilchard when you're
staying in fancy hotels and flying first class."

And this time I don't try to stop him. The warning bell rings, and I consider it a save so I can go
hide in the classroom. What I can't figure out is
how I can be so torn up about leaving and not care
one little bit at the same time.

I stand at the doors of the cafeteria, willing myself
to go in and sit down. At least Bren's will be a
friendly face, but I'm not so sure about the others.
Ashia might finally be ready to talk to me, but I
don't even know what to say to her anymore.

I get the courage to take that first step, when
the last person I want to see walks in front of me
and blocks my way.

"What do you want, Shelby?" I ask, somewhat
curious what the answer is.

"I wanted to thank you for giving the role of

Dorothy back to its rightful owner. Me," she says, as if it wasn't clear enough to begin with. "You and your ridiculous stage fright never would have made it through to the end anyway. We're all better off with you leaving." I want to be the better person here, I really do, but when she throws out those bully moves, I can't stand here and take it.

"Yeah, the only thing is that you aren't the rightful owner," I say. "I was assigned that part because I had a better audition than you did."

"A better audition?" she says. "You mean with the help of a fancy hotel, a pianist, and a yellow brick road? I'm surprised they didn't actually install gold bricks for you."

"I have a good voice," I say. Do I really need to defend myself here?

"You had a whole production put together for you," she says. "I've seen the video."

Could she be right? Maybe they regretted their decision once they heard me sing for real. I'm trying to be strong here, but what if none of this was real at all? What if they were all just interested in what the new girl had to show them? That's what I'll always be no matter where I go—the new girl.

"What? Are you gonna run home to your mommy

now?" Shelby's eyes are cold, and she's standing there like a statue with her arms crossed.

There's so much wrong with that question.

I freeze, trying to decide how to answer. I swear my heart has sunk into my Mary Jane shoes, and the bottoms of my eyes are blurring from the tears fighting their way out. But this is a speak-up-or-slink-away moment, and there is no way I'm letting her keep me down.

"Go ahead, Kenzie. Run home to Mommy," she says again.

I consider thanking her for doing me a favor, because that last dig breaks me out of my haze and puts me in full-out combat mode. I lean forward until our noses are almost touching and lock eyes with her to be sure she understands how bad her words hurt. "I wish more than anything that I still had my mother to run home to."

She clearly doesn't know what to say, and I am not letting her off the hook. "I want you to remember that, because someday your words will run through your mind, you'll picture the sadness you saw in my eyes, and you'll realize what a bully you are."

She backs away from me, trying to act like I didn't get to her, but her shaking hands tell me I did.

"May you never forget this moment," I say as if I'm putting a spell on her. And honestly, it's all I can hope for. That someday she'll understand how cruel it is to knock someone down just to make yourself feel more powerful. No one deserves that.

I turn and walk away as the whispers start. By now everyone knows it's only me and my dad. Apparently, Shelby never got the memo.

"No one told me *that*," she says to her friends. "I didn't *know*."

A tiny little piece of me relaxes, because maybe someday isn't so far off.

chapter twenty-four

Dad suggests going out to dinner tonight, but I want to make sure I have his undivided attention. We compromise and order a pizza. Extra cheese and double the pineapple.

It's one of those movie moments where we both say "I have something to tell you" at the exact same time, and then it continues with "You go first," "No, you go first," until I finally stop him and say, "Dad, I have a whole bunch to tell you, so it's probably better if you tell me what you have to say first."

"Okay, sweetie," he says. "I know traveling all the time is hard for you, and you seem to be having a great time in middle school."

I guess I have more to tell him than I thought. His late nights last week and the birthday celebration this past weekend are clearly hiding how miserable I've been.

"What? Are you not enjoying middle school?" he asks. My face must be giving me away.

"No, I mean, you're going first," I say. "Go on." This time I try to focus with very little expression on my face. I don't want to give away the truth just yet.

"The thing is that the office here is really happy with my work, and it's been a great fit for both sides," says Dad.

I grab another piece of pizza. "That's great, Dad. You're awesome."

He laughs. "Thank you, but that's not the point of the story."

Dad can always make me smile. "Sorry, continue," I say, taking a bite of my pizza.

"They've asked me to stay on longer," he says. His gaze doesn't leave my face, and I can sense he has more to say.

"How long?" I ask.

"Permanently." Dad leans back a little in his chair. "And I said yes."

"What?" I stand up, making my chair screech across the floor. "You mean we're not leaving? Ever?" A month ago, I would have been thrilled with this news, but now? Oh my goodness, this is Bad with a capital *B*.

"I thought you'd be happy," he says, standing up and walking over to me. "Isn't this what you want?"

Dad and I have so much to say to each other. So much to talk about. But right now, the weight of this news is crushing me to the ground and there's only one place I can think of to go for help.

"I know we're supposed to have dinner together and talk about all this, but I wasn't expecting this news—I mean, I wasn't . . ." I take a deep breath and let it out slowly. "Is it okay if I go over to Ashia's?" I ask.

Dad nods. "Yes, of course, whatever you need. We can talk later."

I'm not even sure she'll let me in, and I don't plan on giving her enough warning to be able to hide behind the curtains before I get there. But this is definitely a time when a girl needs a best friend. And while I might have completely lost that privilege, I'm not giving it up without a fight.

* * *

Knock. Knock. Knock. Ding. Dong. I don't want to overdo it, but I want to make sure she gets the urgency of my entrance.

Ashia opens the door slowly. "Kenzie? Is everything okay?"

"Yes, mostly," I say. "Can I come in?"

"Sure." Ashia opens the door farther and steps back, calling down the hall to her mom to let her know I'm there.

"I needed to talk to you before," I say. "But I really need to talk to you now. Please hear me out?"

Ashia motions for me to follow her into the living room, and we sit down on the couch. "What's up?" she asks.

"Well, for starters, I wanted to tell you again how very sorry I am about what I did," I say. "You have every right to be upset or angry or whatever it is you are. But I never intended to hurt anyone. Even though I was sure I'd thought it all through, it turns out my plan wasn't a very smart one."

Ashia's eyes are still on me, and she's making no move to talk, so I continue. "Yes, I get that I have what looks like a very exciting life, but the truth is that it's lonely. I love my dad more than anything, and I do have a lot of fun going to all these places, but I also spend most of my time living in hotels, rushing off to airports, and waiting for my dad to be done with work. It's not as glamorous as it sounds."

"Still, Kenzie, why not say that from the beginning?" asks Ashia.

"I was going to," I say. "But then all these awesome things started coming up, and I was meeting people and making friends, and I wanted to see what life was like without all the special privileges. Here I was just the new girl. I had a totally clean slate to see what I could do. And honestly, I wanted to know how it felt to just be a kid in middle school."

She hasn't yelled at me or thrown me out, so a little bit of hope creeps into my chest.

"Okay, I guess all of that makes sense," she says, as if she's still deciding if it actually does. I stay quiet and let her process it all. "It doesn't make it all right that you didn't tell us, but at least I can understand what you were thinking. I might have done the same thing if I was in your shoes."

I want to reach across the couch and give her an

enormous hug, but I'm not quite sure we're there yet. "Thank you," I say. "And well, there's more." I take a minute to find the right words. "Now I'm not leaving."

She sits back and her eyes widen. "I'm sorry, what?"

"I just had dinner with my dad, and I was about to tell him everything," I say. "I was going to all-out beg him to let us leave early, or at least let me finish school early since . . . well, you know people haven't been all that nice to me lately."

"And?"

"And before I could tell him anything, he said he's accepted a permanent position here. In Vegas. *Permanent*," I repeat to make sure she catches it.

"So now you're staying?" she asks.

"What do I do, Ashia?" I ask. "It's not like I can go back to student council or the musical or even book club. And I'm not exactly anyone's favorite person right now. This is a disaster."

Ashia scoots over and puts an arm around me. "You have to figure out a way to make it right."

I reach my hand up and grab hers. "Will you help me?" I ask.

She takes her arm off, but stays close, facing

me. "Listen, I forgive you, okay? But that doesn't mean everything is instantly fixed. I'm not sure I even know how to feel about you staying. And I'm really not sure how I can help you right now anyway."

I nod, although it's not completely clear what she's getting at. Just that I'm pretty much on my own.

I don't have much of a choice. "Okay."

She walks me to the door and gives me a hug, but it's not the kind I need. It's not a Dad hug that says *Everything's going to be okay.* And it's certainly not a Mom hug that says *I'll love you no matter what.*

But I'll take it. Because it's at least an *I'm here if you need me* hug.

chapter twenty-five

On the morning that should have meant four more days to go before we left, I'm back in school. My school. The one I'll be going to now—permanently. That word sticks in my mind, constantly keeping my heart beating a little faster. Because "permanently" could have been a good thing, but now it means I'm stuck here.

Stuck.

Here.

Dad and I are never stuck anywhere unless there's a massive storm and all flights are canceled. But eventually, it's time to go. Not this time.

So what does a girl do when she's lost most of

her friends, no longer has any activities to participate in, and the cutest boy in school (who once *liked* her) now avoids her at all costs? I don't know yet, but I'm determined to figure something out.

In English, I say hi to Bren but manage not to say any more. I can't bear to find out how he feels about the news that I'm staying. Yes, he said he'd miss me, but maybe he only said it because I was leaving. Just like all the things I did because I didn't think I'd have to face the consequences.

At the end of class, when Mrs. Pilchard casually mentions that students are needed for several school activities, I beeline for the sheet with the info, not caring that everyone is probably wondering why on earth I'd need that information. One of the activities stands out right away, and I'm sure it's the answer.

I skip the lunchroom and my hiding spot in the library and instead go in search of Mr. Mason. He makes it pretty easy, since he's in the computer lab right where the sheet said he'd be.

"Excuse me?" I poke my head in the doorway. "Mr. Mason?"

He swivels his chair to face me. "Hi there. What can I do for you?"

I step inside. "I'm Kenzie Rhines. I don't know if you've heard about me." Might as well get it out in the open.

"Oh yes, I might have heard a little something," he says, standing up. "But no worries. You're obviously here for a reason. Have a seat."

I sit down on one of the hard plastic seats and Mr. Mason plants himself back in his chair.

"I've been taking some photography lessons, and I was wondering if maybe I could be part of the yearbook team," I say.

His face suddenly looks confused.

"Oh, right, because you think I'm leaving," I say. "But I'm not."

The look of confusion doesn't change. "I thought that was what caused all the commotion—that you're leaving."

"It is," I say, "but things have changed, and, well, now everyone is stuck with me."

"You're not leaving anymore?" he asks.

"Nope," I answer. "So can I join the yearbook team?"

He takes some papers out of his desk drawer. "Yes, I think that would be wonderful. Here are some assignments we need covered."

And the first one on the list? Musical rehearsals. Second? Book club. Great.

"I'll take these two," I say. Because at this point,
why not? "I can start tomorrow."

"Perfect," says Mr. Mason. "Are you all set with
a camera? We have some for students, but honestly, a lot of them use their phones."

I pull out my phone and show him some of
the photos I took in Washington. "These were
taken with my other camera. I had a lesson with
Kuan-yin—"

"Kuan-yin *Fei*?" Mr. Mason is gripping the sides
of his chair.

"Yes, do you know him?" I ask.

He laughs. "He's kind of a famous photographer, Kenzie. Did you really have a lesson from
him?"

"Yeah, he's a friend of my dad's," I say. "We're
all set, then?"

Mr. Mason smiles. "If you've been trained by
Kuan-yin Fei, I'd say you'll do fine on a middle-
school yearbook committee."

"Thanks, Mr. Mason," I say. And this time, I

don't even care that once again, my VIP privileges are helping me along. Because if they help me survive this school year, so be it.

My enthusiasm for my new assignment on the yearbook team doesn't last very long. On Wednesday after school, I decide to split my time between taking pictures at musical rehearsal and book club. I don't even tell anyone I'm coming. I sneak in the back of the auditorium and make my way toward the stage. I stop and move down one of the middle rows until I get to a point where I can get a good photo of the Cowardly Lion, the Tin Man, the Scarecrow, and the new Dorothy—Shelby.

I manage to snap a few great ones and pull the camera down to adjust some of the controls when my name echoes throughout the room. "Kenzie?! What is she doing here?" Shelby can't help herself.

Mrs. Summers puts up a hand to Shelby. "Let's all take a short break, and I'll handle this." She walks over to me. "Kenzie, honey, these are now closed rehearsals. We need the cast to focus."

"Oh, I know," I say, but she doesn't let me finish.

"And given the circumstances, you should

respect that your presence here is very distract-
ing," says Mrs. Summers.

"But I—" I hold up the camera, but it doesn't
make one bit of difference.

"I'm so sorry, but I think it's time to leave," she
says.

Oh, Mrs. Summers, it's always time for me to
leave. Except this *time, when I desperately wish*
I could.

But I don't say another word. I pack up my camera and make my way down to the library, where
book club is meeting. Here goes nothing.

It's a much smaller group, so there's no way I can
sneak in here unnoticed and start snapping pictures. "Hi, guys," I say. "I'm here on yearbook duty."

They give me the same look Mr. Mason did. "Oh,
right, well, see, that whole leaving thing? It's actually not happening." I put a hand in the air and
strike a pose. "Surprise." I intentionally leave the
usual enthusiasm out of my surprise, since I'm
fairly certain it's not a good one.

Bren stands up. "You're *staying*?" It's almost
as if he's trying to stop the sides of his lips from
arching into a smile.

I nod.

"She's staying? Oh man," says Paul, who is probably wondering if he'll have to go back to being co–vice president again. "I can't keep track of this drama." He shakes his head and flops it on the table.

Divi doesn't say anything and I can't quite read her expression. Confusion? Shock? Bren gently grabs my arm and guides me to the hallway. When we're out of sight of the others, he lets the smile go full force. "What happened?" he asks.

For the first time since Dad told me, I get a little flicker of happiness that I'll still be here after Friday. Not enough to make me want to stay, but still. "My dad was offered a job here," I say. "And he took it."

Bren takes a step back and puts his hands in his pockets. "So how do you feel about that?"

I don't know how to answer. I feel stuck. I can't believe I have to stay here forever. Permanently. But now I'm standing here in front of Bren, and, well, maybe it's not as bad as I'm making it out to be. "I'm not sure," I say.

"Why don't you think about it and let me know," says Bren. He points to the camera. "Didn't take you long to jump back into activities."

"Oh yeah, well, I'm going a little stir-crazy not having anything to do."

"Ah, got it. Although you might want to wait until next week to try popping into book club again. Give everyone a little time to get used to the idea of you staying." He heads back through the library door and waves. "See you later, sunshine."

And whether I want to or not, I smile.

chapter twenty-six

think about Bren's question all night. How *do* I feel about staying?

There's Bren, of course, and there's a chance Ashia and I could be friends again. I have no idea what Divi is thinking. But the others? I'm pretty sure it's a lost cause. And I'll never be able to audition for the musical again or run for student council. I've pretty much made it impossible to enjoy middle school from this point on.

So I make a decision. A big one. To convince Dad that staying here is not a good idea. It's a bad idea. A very, very bad idea.

I get out my laptop and open up a presentation program. I'm always making these for Dad's assignments, so this will be a no-brainer. I've done enough pros-and-cons lists to earn myself an honorary degree.

I set up the slides with the most professional-looking templates I can find, keeping nice, bright colors on the pro slides and leaving dark, gloomy colors on the cons side. I'll take any help I can get to convince him that staying isn't the answer.

The first slide states my topic:

LEAVING LAS VEGAS

The second slide presents my first argument:

PRO: first class; CON: not applicable

I jot down a few notes on a piece of paper, trying to get my thoughts in order to make this something he can't say no to.

PRO: see the world (let's go international!);
CON: try to find one—seriously

I make eight more slides, whipping through them and coming up with more and more pros as I go. Nice hotels, VIP treatment, fun events, different foods, and one I know will get him—spending more time together.

On the last slide, which I'm sure will convince him, I add:

> **PRO: seeing friends—Fiona, Kuan-yin and Mayleen, Genevieve; CONS:**

I stop, because this is the first one where I can't put a "not applicable." The first one I can't skim over like it doesn't matter. *Type it, Kenzie*, I tell myself. Except that once I do, it's real. It's out in the world, in print, admitting that there is a big fat CON to leaving this place. And if there's anything I've learned about a pros-and-cons list, is that it's not about the *number* of things on each side; it's about the things on each side that can't be measured by numbers.

> **CON: leaving my friends**

I stare at it for a minute, letting the hugeness of it hit me. And then I scroll back through the slides to *PRO: nice hotels* and make a change.

CON: they're not a home

I don't even attempt to go to musical rehearsal on Thursday, and since it's a week until book club, my yearbook duties are on hold anyway. I plan another big-talk dinner with Dad and even ask Alexandria to help me make dinner. I pick Dad's favorite— three-cheese lasagna—and between the two of us, we manage to bake something that at least smells pretty good. The table is all made up when Dad gets home, and the warm scent of noodles and cheese fills the kitchen.

"What's this all about?" asks Dad after Alexandria leaves.

"I wanted to do something special," I say. As I pull the lasagna out of the oven, it hits me that having our own oven to cook in—even having things like noodles and cheese around to cook with—might have been something on the pro list if I were lobbying to stay.

I bring my laptop over from the counter and set up the presentation.

"What's going on, Kenzie? Is everything all right?" asks Dad.

I hit the start button. "It will be. If you say yes to

my proposal." The screen lights up with my cover slide.

"Leaving Las Vegas?" says Dad. "Kenzie—"

But I cut him off. I've worked very hard on this, and one way or another I'm finally going to tell Dad what's been going on. "Please, Dad, just let me do this," I say.

He gives me a nod to continue.

"A lot has been going on at school that I haven't told you about," I say. "The truth is that I *don't* love it here, and I miss being in the air and on the road with you. So I'm asking that you please, please, please consider my suggestion that you keep your job and we go back to our old life."

I can tell I have my work cut out for me when Dad gives me that lips-pushed-together look, complete with head tilt.

I start with pro number one and by the time I get to number five—tickets to live-audience shows anytime we want—Dad is smiling.

"We do have a lot of fun with all the traveling, huh?" he says.

"We really do," I answer. Before I lose momentum, I move on to the next slide. Dad laughs at some of my cons, and I'm sure it's pretty clear this is a totally biased list. Of course, it's meant to be. But when we get to what I now call the friends slide, I do my best to hurry past it.

"Hold on a minute," says Dad. "That looks like a pretty important one."

I flip back to it, but don't say a word.

"If we were to go, and I'm not saying we are, you'd be leaving your friends behind," says Dad. "Do you understand that?"

"I do," I say. "But we have friends all over. And now I have Mayleen."

"Yes, but Mayleen lives in Washington, and we'd be living . . ." He stops and lowers his head. "We'd be living nowhere, sweetheart. I've asked so much of you these last few years, but now I can give you a real home. Don't you want that?"

I sit down and push the laptop to the side. "It's just that . . ." I stop, not ready to finish the sentence.

"What is it, Kenzie?" asks Dad. "You can tell me anything."

I try to take a deep breath, but my chest does that staccato thing it does when your body is trying to cry and breathe at the same time. "Dad, the last time I had a home . . . Mom was in it." I've done my best to put on a professional (although biased) front, but it's time to get real with my dad. I don't even try to hold back the tears that are now busting their way out.

"Oh, honey, I'm so sorry." Dad gets out of his chair and kneels down in front of me, taking my hands. "If I could change what happened, I'd do it in a heartbeat. But right now, the only thing I can change is what you have moving forward."

I grab a napkin and wipe at my eyes. "I don't have what you think I do, Dad."

He waits patiently for me to elaborate.

"I didn't tell anyone I was leaving," I say. "I let them think I had actually moved here, and I tried out for the lead in the musical even though I knew I wouldn't be here for the show." As the words come out of my mouth, I understand that this one fact alone is bad enough, and Dad confirms it.

"Can I ask why you'd do that?" he says.

I wipe at my eyes again. "I wanted to be a regular kid," I say. "To do middle-school things and be a part of it all. I thought it was the only chance I'd ever have."

Dad pulls his chair over close to me and sits down. "Go on."

"I got the lead, and I still didn't say anything. I went to practices like nothing was wrong," I say. "And then Ashia wanted me to run for student council as her vice president, and it sounded fun and I didn't want to let her down, so I did it. And I got that, too. Sort of. It was a tie, and this kid Tate won for president too."

"And who is Tate?" asks Dad.

"Yeah, that's a whole other story. On my first day, I actually told the kid he was cute," I say. "Do you believe that? Me, Kenzie Rhines, I got all bold and brave because I knew—I mean, I thought—I'd never have to face any of them again after we left. It was like a free pass to try out all the rides and then go home and forget it ever happened."

I'm relieved to finally be telling Dad the truth. I can't imagine he'll be anything but disappointed in me, but at least it's all out there.

"Did they find out?" he asks.

"They sure did," I say. "This girl Shelby had it out for me from day one, and she overheard me coming clean to Ashia. Then I wrote this letter and I was going to tell everyone the truth before she did, but apparently she couldn't wait another day to ruin my life."

"I wish you'd told me," says Dad. "And maybe I should have told you sooner about the possibility of staying here."

I sit up straight, clutching the napkin. "You *knew* we might not be leaving?"

"That's why I took on this project, because the potential for a permanent position was there," he says. "I never mentioned it because I didn't want to get your hopes up. I'm so sorry, Kenzie. It didn't occur to me that you wouldn't tell people our situation."

I run through this whole mess in my mind. "That's why Mr. Kumar didn't know," I say, putting it all together. "Because you figured we'd be staying."

"Yes," says Dad. "I mean, there was a good chance we'd be staying. But I guess I should have mentioned our situation just in case."

There's a part of me that's so, so mad right now. If he'd only told me that from the beginning, I wouldn't be in this mess. But the rational side of me is reminding me that *I'm* the one who caused this problem and there's no one else to blame.

"I shouldn't have hidden the truth. This is all my fault, and now I'm stuck in this place where no one wants anything to do with me."

Dad grabs a tissue box off the counter and hands it to me. Much better idea than the napkins. He leans back in his chair with a faraway look in his eyes.

I give him a minute, so whatever is going through his head can work itself out.

He takes my hands again. "Listen, sweetheart. The first time we left home, I didn't give you a choice. I needed my job to support us, and honestly, I convinced myself that leaving was the best thing. I thought a new adventure might be good for both of us, and I wanted to be with you as much as possible. But you should have had a say."

I focus on Dad. Not just on his words, but on his face and his eyes, which are so full of both pain and love right now. I focus on his shoulders, slumped but strong.

"So I'm giving you the choice this time," he says. "It's up to you, Kenzie. If you want to stay, we'll stay. But if you want to go . . ."

I wait for him to complete the sentence to be sure he's saying what I think he's saying.

"Then we'll go," he finishes.

And now, with the decision completely in my hands, I have no idea what to do.

chapter twenty-seven

Today is supposed to be my last day of
school. Bags should be packed to leave this
place tomorrow. But Dad has given me the
weekend to make a decision. To make the biggest
decision of my life.

We'll leave after school for Orlando, which
means a stop at Disney World is definitely on the
agenda.

At school, though, nobody knows that. Now
they all think I'm staying; they don't know
there's a choice to be made. Do I tell them? Would
anyone even care? Most of them would probably
make the choice easily for me—they'd tell me
to go. But in order to make the right decision, I

need all the information. A real pros-and-cons list that isn't secretly a way to convince Dad one way or the other.

In English class, I don't avoid Bren. Instead I turn around and act like nothing is wrong.

"Hey, you never told me what happened last year with the election posters," I say.

He leans forward and whispers. "Oh, right. We call it the Mustache Incident."

With a tell-all title like that, I don't even need to ask for more details, but I want to keep the conversation going. "The Mustache Incident?"

"Somebody decided all the posters needed some sprucing up," he says. "There were even red eyes and top hats. Candidates were *not* happy with their new looks."

"So that's why posters aren't allowed up early," I say, finally understanding. "Because of a rogue group of mustache-drawing vandals."

Bren and I laugh, a little too loudly, apparently, getting a shush from the girls next to us.

After class I ask Mrs. Pilchard if there's still a chance I might be able to read my poem at the awards dinner. I don't give her the latest update when she says, "Yes, I heard the good news that you'll be staying with us." I might have told her that I still need to make that decision if she hadn't used the word "good" to describe the news, but I decide to enjoy the moment.

When it's time for lunch, I go to the caf. My days of hiding out in the library are done.

"Hi, everyone," I say. "Is it okay if I sit here?" I'm more than surprised when most of them smile and say yes.

"Wasn't sure you'd be back," says Bren.

For a second, I wonder if he knows about the choice I have to make. "What do you mean?" I ask.

"Thought we'd lost you to the library at lunch-time," he says with a chuckle.

"Ah, got it," I say. "Have I missed any interesting performances?" There hasn't been any spontaneous singing in several weeks, and I'm afraid I might be jinxing myself. As much as I'm pretty sure I don't want Tate singing to *me*, I certainly don't want to see him singing to another girl either.

"Nope, nothing to report," says Ashia. "Are you going anywhere this weekend? A bunch of us were thinking of seeing a movie."

I run her words through my mind again, but yes, that was definitely an invite to hang out with everyone. Maybe things could get better here. Having friends to go to movies with would be a plus for sure.

"I'd love to, but yeah, Dad and I will be in Orlando this weekend," I say.

"Lu-cky," says one of the girls.

"Wish I could hop off to Orlando this weekend," says another.

The rest of lunch goes fine, if you don't count all the looks I'm getting from some of the seventh graders, but it still doesn't feel right. It's like I'm walking around in some world that isn't mine. Like I'm an impostor trying to fit in. And I wonder if this place could ever be a real home for me and Dad.

It's kind of hard to think about anything else when you're at the top of the Tower of Terror and you know the floor's about to drop, sending you many, many stories down at warp speed. Dad grabs my hand.

"You ready?" he asks, knowing as well as I do that the "terror" is only seconds away.

Right as the floor comes out from under us, everyone on the ride goes silent, except for one girl, who picks that exact moment to yell out, "I've never been so scared in my life!" making all the riders do a mix of both laughing and screaming on the way down.

"Let's do it again!" I say to Dad when it's over.

He laughs. "Can we take a break? I'm not as young as I used to be."

I sit on a nearby bench, and Dad goes to get us a couple of waters. While I'm waiting, two completely separate things go through my mind because, somehow, they fit together: *I've never been so scared in my life* and *I'm not as young as I used to be.*

There isn't much that could compete with my never-been-so-scared moment; being afraid of losing my mom tops everything. But as next most scared? I'd say being afraid of making the wrong choice right now is totally a nominee. And, sure, I'm too young to be using Dad's line, but I won't ever be this age again. I won't ever have the chance to do twelve-year-old things when I'm older. But this life with Dad? Disney World and NYC and, maybe, if I can convince him, Venice and Barcelona? Not many kids my age get to do that, either.

Dad and I spend the rest of the day, the *entire*

day, going from one ride to another. We even park
hop a couple times.

On Sunday, I sleep in until noon. Because whatever world I choose to live in, that is definitely
something preteens get to do on the weekend.
When I make my way to the dining area (they've
upgraded us to their best suite), there's a catering
tray full of breakfast and lunch choices for me. I
actually don't like when they do this—it must be
a new concierge—because Dad and I can't stand
wasting the food we don't eat. I pick the pancakes
with a side of fruit and call down to the desk to
have them send someone up to bring the food to
their hungriest employees who haven't had a lunch
break yet. "No, no, I insist. Check with Philippe;
he knows." I sit down to eat, and it's super quiet.
Like, no music playing on a chaperone's iPod, no
one chatting on the phone. I get up and check out
one room at a time (part of the problem with having more than one room in a hotel), but there's no
one anywhere. No one. Dad never leaves me alone
at a hotel.

"Dad?" I call. No answer. I peek into the hall.
"Dad?" I step out, careful not to let the door close
behind me.

"Excuse me?" The voice behind me startles me so much that I let go of the door. I reach for it, but I'm not quick enough to catch it before it locks shut. It's a girl, maybe a couple of years younger than I am.

"Can I help you with something?" I ask her.

"I was actually wondering if I could help you," she says. "I'm next door and I heard you calling for your dad."

Just as I'm wondering where her parents are, a woman sticks her head out the door. "Everything okay?" she asks.

"I was looking for my dad," I say. "And now I've locked the door and I don't have a key." This is what I mean when I say life on the road isn't as glamorous as it looks. I lock myself out, and instead of going next door to get a spare key from a friend, my next-door neighbor is a hotel guest and total stranger.

The woman steps into the hall. "Would it help to call him? You can use my cell phone."

"Yes, thank you." I take the phone and dial Dad's number, and his ringtone echoes through the hall immediately. Within seconds, there's Dad with a bucket of ice and three hotel employees offering to carry it for him.

"Kenzie, you're up," he says. "I'm so sorry—I stepped out for a few minutes to get some ice. I didn't want to wake you."

As if Cinderella herself is parading down the hallway, Dad stops and stares. "Oh, hello," he says to the girl's mom. "I'm Brian, and this is my daughter, Kenzie."

She introduces herself as Catherine and her daughter as Jolene. And as the three of them laugh at something Dad says, I can't believe it hasn't ever occurred to me that maybe Dad needs a home so he can make new friends and move forward too.

chapter twenty-eight

We ended up having dinner with our new hotel friends Catherine and Jolene. They were both so nice, and to be honest, it was pretty amazing to see Dad smiling and laughing like he was.

Now we're sitting in the airport, on our way, well, home? Or is it just back to Vegas?

My phone needs a charge, so I plug it into the outlet, and it immediately lets me know I have new messages.

There's one from Mayleen. Have you made a decision?

One from Ashia. Hey, friend. Hope you're having fun.

And one from Bren. What time does your flight get in?

I answer them one at a time.

Nope. Someone I need to talk to first.

Very fun weekend. Can't wait to see you. And I quickly realize it could be the very last time I see her.

7 tonight.

I attempt to text back and forth with all three of them, but eventually the announcement comes on that they'll be preboarding, so I pack everything up.

"How are all your friends?" asks Dad.

"They're good," I say. "Turns out not *everyone* hates me."

"I figured that might be the case," he says.

"Dad?" I wait for him to answer to make sure I have his complete attention.

"Yes, honey?" he says as he stuffs a magazine in his suitcase.

"You said I didn't get a choice, but I did," I say.

He stops zipping his bag and turns to me. "What do you mean?"

"I choose all the time," I answer. "Which city to go to next. The hotel we're going to stay in. What activities to do. You're always thinking of what I want."

"That's what dads do for their daughters," he says.

And I know the conversation could stop right here. I could decide whatever I want and Dad would do it, for me. But if there's anything I've learned in the last six weeks, it's that this isn't just about me.

"What do *you* want, Dad?" I ask. "Do you want to stay in Vegas or do you want to leave?"

"It's not my decision to make, Kenzie," he says without a second thought.

"I know. You've left it up to me. But in order to make the right decision, I need to know how you feel about the whole thing," I say. I repeat my question: "What do *you* want?"

He smiles and taps me on the nose like he did when I was a little kid. "Honestly? I think it could be a really good thing for us to stay," he says. "But what I want more than anything is for you to be happy. For you to feel like you're getting everything you need in life. So whatever—and wherever—that is, that's what I want too."

I lean over and hug my dad like I haven't seen him in years. And I don't let go until they call us to board.

While we're on the plane, I let everything run through my mind. All of it.

My old house. Neighborhood. Friends.

Our life in the air. The hotels. All the cities. Our friends on the road.

And Vegas. It could either be our new life, or it could be the one we leave behind and maybe only think about every once in a while.

I've been living in two different worlds at the same time. There's one world where everyone gives me anything I need, but I'm constantly on the go. And there's another one where I'd have to fight for what I want, but I'd finally have a chance at a real home again.

When the captain comes on with the usual announcement about landing soon and local weather, I'm pretty sure I know what I want to do, but one little part of me is holding back. Am I sure?

When the Vegas strip and all the mountains come into view through my window, I'm *almost* positive I've made my choice.

And when the plane touches down, the captain makes his announcement: "Welcome to Las Vegas, folks. If this is a stop on your journey, we wish you safe travels. If this is your final destination, enjoy your trip. And for those of you heading back to friends and family . . . welcome home."

That's when I know for sure.

"I've made my decision," I say to Dad.

chapter twenty-nine

Ashia and Bren are the only ones I tell that I had a choice, and I chose to stay.

"So you picked us," says Ashia on Monday morning as we stand in the hallway. "Over Disney World and yellow brick roads and movie premieres. You picked us." She's smiling from ear to ear, and I couldn't be more thrilled that she's happy about the news.

"Yes," I say. "Although Dad says we can still do that stuff every once in a while. He has a ton of travel points, and connections are connections, you know?"

Ashia gives me a giant hug, and while I know

I still have a lot to make up to her, we're on the right track.

Bren is quiet, and I'm so scared he's changed his mind. That maybe he only *thought* he'd miss me, but now that I'm here, he's wishing I'd decided to leave.

"Bren?" I ask. "Is this okay?" Not that I'm prepared to change my mind or have Dad say no to his new position at this point—the decision has been made. But I need Bren to be on board with this. I don't know why, but his opinion is the last piece of this puzzle.

His face doesn't give me any hint of what he's thinking. I turn to Ashia, who gives me a shrug and a silent *I can never figure him out.*

"Bren, say something." I tap him on the shoulder. "Please tell me you're not wishing I was leaving after all." I'm positive I'm a stronger version of who I was six weeks ago, but he's making it hard to stand here and wait.

His lips crack into a small smile. "I'm trying to find the right words," he says.

Bren is at a loss for words? Well, that's something new.

"If you'd left," he says, and stops. "Kenzie, if

you'd left, I would have lost a friend, and so, no, I'm definitely not wishing that. I'm wishing I had the courage to hug you right now."

I summon up my brave and bold, step over to Bren, and whip my arms around him. He squeezes tight—one of those hugs that says so much without any words at all.

When I let go, Shelby and Tate stare at me from down at the end of the hall. I wave.

"I have a little work to do to apologize to everyone around here, and I was hoping you'd help me," I say to Ashia and Bren.

They both agree, and for the first time in this whole adventure, I walk to what is most definitely *my* homeroom, in *my* school, with *my* friends.

chapter thirty

spend the next week doing two things. One, making things right. And two, begging Mrs. Summers and the student council to hear me out. All week long, I take my pictures, insisting that I am official yearbook staff and these are important assignments. I'm ready to face whatever wrath is coming at me.

On Friday, Mrs. Summers finds me after school and asks if I can stay for rehearsal. "I can't give you back the role of Dorothy," she says, "but if you're willing to be in the chorus, we'd love to have you."

I'm so excited about what she's saying, but I do have one question before I say yes. "Is the cast okay with me coming back? Because I can't do it if I'm going to upset everyone by being there."

She smiles. "Yes, we took a vote and it was an almost unanimous decision to let you come back," she says. When my face scrunches into a *Yeah, that must be my nemesis who voted no* face, she laughs. "Shelby said, and I quote, 'If you're saying I am the star and she has to settle for dancing in the shadows, then sure.'"

I have to laugh too, because quite honestly, I expected nothing less from the girl. We'll have to learn to exist on this planet together eventually. Especially if I decide to try out for the lead in next year's musical.

And Friday night, I get a text from Tate.

Need note taker when secretary can't make meetings. You interested?

I can't expect a smiley face at the end of that text, but at least there isn't a thumbs-down.

Yes. Thank you.

Don't thank me, he texts back.

Well, you can't win them all.

I spend the next few weeks continuing to make it up to everyone, and working hard in every role I've been given. Dad has one more weekend away before he settles into his new job, which he's very excited about. And that makes me the kind of happy that makes everything in the world better.

On the plane ride back from Chicago, I relax in my seat, both a little sad and a whole lot of happy that this is the last adventure for a while. Yeah, I'm okay with that.

When we get to the airport, I'm surrounded by busy travelers rolling their suitcases along the shiny floor, and all I can think is that life is kind of like an airport. Plenty of people will land in your life, and others will take off to new destinations for one reason or another. Some flights won't matter much at all, just another listing on the screen, while some departures will break your heart into a million tiny pieces that only time can heal. But then there are the delays that maybe are the best thing you didn't even know you needed.

We're about halfway down the escalator on the way to baggage claim when I look up to a big surprise.

Ashia, Bren, and Divi are waiting at the bottom, holding bright, colorful signs—signs for me!

WE MISSED YOU!

SO GLAD YOU'RE BACK!

WELCOME HOME, KENZIE!

In all the time Dad and I have been on the road (or, really, up in the air), we've never gotten this kind of greeting. I'm practically dancing as I run down the last few steps toward my friends.

"What are you guys doing here?" I ask.

They all laugh. "We figured you deserved a little welcoming party," says Ashia. "Plus, we wanted to make sure it was just a weekend trip and that you're back for good."

I let her words sink in.

Home isn't about a pin on a map. It's the place you can't wait to get back to after you've been away. It's the *people* you can't wait to get back to, even after your biggest adventure.

I take another look at the poster-board signs, and as I stand here, carry-on bag slung over my shoulder, I'm more sure than ever that this is where I want to be.

Welcome home, Kenzie.

Acknowledgments

Pieces of my experiences, as well as traits of the people I've met, often find their way into my stories. But unlike Kenzie, I've never had to search for a place to call home. Thank you, Buffalo, for truly being the City of Good Neighbors. There really is no place like home.

Thank you to my agent extraordinaire, Uwe Stender, whom I snagged with sponge candy and *Seinfeld* references one fateful day in Pittsburgh. I couldn't have predicted that a tall German with a sense of humor and a tiger-toughness would be the one helping make my dreams come true, but I wouldn't have it any other way.

Thank you to my editor, Alyson Heller, who

not only makes my stories take shape, but who also will hop in a shopping cart to re-create my cover in the Wegmans parking lot. This awesomeness can't be found just anywhere, folks. Thank you from the bottom of my heart for being such a big part of my books' finding their way to the shelves.

Thank you to the entire Aladdin team, including Jessica Handelman and Rebecca Vitkus. You all amaze me with your talents. And Annabelle Metayer, who illustrates the most beautiful covers I could ever ask for.

I'm so grateful for my writing communities and writer friends—BNCWI, RACWI, The Guild, The Sweet Sixteens, You've Got This, SCBWI, and Team Triada (You too, Brent Taylor!). And my writing group (even if we sometimes talk more than write), Adrienne Carrick, Claudia Seldeen, Kate Karyus Quinn, Sandi van Everdingen, Jenn Kompos, and Alyssa Palombo.

To my writing buddies who have been along for the ride and still stick with me—Summer Heacock, Triona Murphy, Kim Chase, Brenda Drake, Heather Cashman, Stephanie Wass, Jessica Collins, Jenny Lundquist, Dana Edwards, Pam Brunskill, Erica

Secor, Rhonda Battenfelder—and my BNE crew, Stephanie Faris, Ronni Arno, Gail Nall, Alison Cherry, Rachele Alpine. Nancy Eckerson and Terri Skurzewski for your smiles and support whenever I need them. And to Catherine Dowling, who definitely deserved to have her name in a book and never got the chance.

For this book specifically, and for a million other reasons, thank you to Janet Johnson, Jennifer Maschari, and Jen Malone. You ladies are sprinkled throughout everything I do, and I'm so grateful to have you by my side.

Thank you to Fiona Ash for quickly making the fictional Fiona exactly who I needed her to be. (And to John, because you both deserve thanks for the many things you've done for me!) Thank you, Amy Teal, for answering my school musical questions, Kristin Rae for my wonderful bookmarks, Gaby Zapata for your beautiful design work, and David Etkin and the SH Middle crew for making such fun book trailers! To Ilene Franz for being one of those people who inspires me every time we talk, and Barbara Marale for encouraging a young writer in third grade when I got my first issue of *Panther's Pause* and dreamed of publishing a book someday.

And to some amazing librarians—Heidi Ginal, Christina Carter, Janice Cosenza, and Brandon Morrisey, for your continued support and for fostering a love of reading in kids.

A huge thank-you to my kid readers for *The BFF Bucket List*. I hope you enjoy this one too. Tyler, Brooke, Ava, Paul, Camryn, Drew, Madison, Novalee, Malaina, Caitlin, Sahana, Lola, Jing-Lu, Lucia, Hannah, Kiersten, Eliana, Jessica, Isabella, Cecilia, Allison Marie, Lorelei, Madigan, Sammy, Nora, Maddie, Brenna, Giuliana, Chiara, Lea, Shaina, Ashley, Raye, Jami, Macie, Manhasset Public Library Tween Girls Book Club, South Davis Elementary School's fifth grade, and Dodge Elementary.

To my wonderful local booksellers at Monkey See, Monkey Do—Kim Krug, Kathleen Skoog, Kim Burg, Amy Nash, Kathy Witter—and Kim and Mike at the Amherst B&N. I really appreciate your support!

My favorite writing spots—the Audubon Library, Wegmans, Barnes & Noble, and Spot Coffee—thank you for giving me places to write that are surrounded by books and food!

To the schools, kids, and teachers who continue to influence my writing. Thank you, Coronation Drive friends, Sweet Home Middle, East

Side Elementary, Riverview Elementary, Heim Elementary, and my Maplemere crew. Who knew that all we went through in sixth grade would become writing material someday?

To my friends—those of you I've known most of my life, and those I've met along the way—I cherish our friendships and thank you for all your support. You all mean the world to me.

Thank you to Anne, who helped me get the ending just right because it was my turn for "What's another word for . . . ?" To Ankur for being the best host and for always being excited for me. To my FLGT girls—Wendy, Sara, Allison, Jen, Christine, Sabrina, Amy Romus—thank you isn't enough to let you know how much I love you all.

To my family, which extends to places like Rochester, Canada, and Virginia, to name a few. Thank you for your support and encouragement. I am blessed to have you.

To my dad, Bill, who keeps buying my books and giving them away to his friends, who reads middle-grade because his daughter wrote it, who watches his grandkids while I write, and who has always made me believe in myself because I watched him go after his goals. I love you.

To my incredible mother, Sandy. She believed in me, cheered me on, and always encouraged me to do what I love. I miss you every single day, Mom, and I will take your lessons and your kindness with me wherever I go.

Thank you to my husband, Rob, who listens when I talk about characters and plot points and gives me his feedback, even if I don't always use it. I love sharing our adventures together.

To Moira, Christine, and Adrienne, whom I officially declare my sisters. You have steered me through so much. And to make you smile like you always do for me—Moira: root beer; Adrienne: Red River; Christine: St. Patty's Day. I love you ladies.

To my kids, Nathan and Kiley. I love watching you as you devour books, write your own stories, and create beautiful pieces of art. Be bold and brave. I love you.

TURN THE PAGE
FOR A PEEK AT
BEST. NIGHT. EVER.

BEST. NIGHT. EVER.

A STORY TOLD FROM SEVEN POINTS OF VIEW

CARMEN { **6:00 P.M.** }

USUALLY LYNNFIELD MIDDLE SCHOOL'S gym smells like sweaty socks and armpits.

But tonight, everything is different.

Tonight, the gym smells like perfume, hairspray, and the pizza that everyone devoured right away. And instead of getting pelted in the face during a vicious game of dodgeball or doing a million jumping jacks, my friends and I are about to make history when we perform our band's hit song, "Hear Us Roar."

The room buzzes with excitement. Our classmates gather at the makeshift stage the drama club constructed, some pushing to get as close as possible, others taking selfies in front of the giant sign the decorating committee hung up with our name, Heart Grenade, written across it.

Suddenly the room goes dark and the audience erupts in cheers. This is it. Our moment!

A single spotlight turns on, illuminating me.

I look out into the crowd and soak up the moment as my classmates' shouts wash over me. I picture myself as they might. My long black hair is flat-ironed sleek and shiny, and the light from above draws attention to my red streaks. My satin dress poofs out at the bottom, and the short white leather jacket looks amazing over it. I have on Mom's vintage biker boots with the big silver buckles, and hot pink tights add the perfect touch. I'm rocker cute, as my best friend, Tess, likes to say.

"Hello, Lynnfield Middle School!" I yell into the microphone. The sound of my voice sweeps through the gym. "We're Heart Grenade, and we're ready to rock!"

Tess starts playing the drums, Faith comes in on the bass, and as Claudia launches into her signature guitar riff, the lights go up over the whole band, and our classmates go wild.

I open my mouth to start singing . . . and something soft smacks me in the head.

"Ouch!"

And just like that I'm jolted out of the best daydream ever and back into the worst reality ever. Because instead of being in the middle school gym performing with Heart Grenade like I'm supposed to be tonight, I'm surrounded by beige-and-maroon-striped wallpaper in a very tiny and very crowded hotel room with my family.

My eyes land on my ten-year-old brother, Lucas. He's dressed in a gray suit that's too short for him, and his dark hair is all spiky, even though Mom told him it would be really nice if he just combed it straight. But his appearance isn't what I care about; it's what is in his hands. He's holding Pandy, my bear that I *may* still sleep with, although I'd never admit that to anyone. He dances around me and dangles Pandy in front of my face.

I yank her away from him. "Get your grubby hands off of my bear."

"Gladly. I've got some reading to do anyway." Lucas pulls my diary from under his pillow on the bed.

"Give me that!" I reach to grab the notebook with the hand that isn't holding Pandy, but he pulls it away from me. I have no idea how the little sneak got hold of it, since I packed it deep down into my duffel bag, but there's no way I'm letting him see what's inside. He'd never let me live down the pages I filled about how cute my bandmate Claudia's brother is.

"Mooooom," I yell, but she waves a hand at me. She's talking on the phone in rapid-fire Spanish to my aunt Sonia, or "the mother of the bride," as everyone keeps saying, and is trying to convince her that something to do with the flowers is going to be all right. But meanwhile, this diary situation most certainly is not going to turn out all right.

I tackle Lucas and thankfully wrestle the notebook away from him, but not before getting an elbow to the gut and a knee to my head.

"You'd better sleep with one eye open," I warn him. "I'm not going to forget this."

"Ohhhh, I'm so scared," he replies and rolls his eyes.

"You look like Christmas," my seven-year-old brother, Alex, says, and my attention shifts to him. Yep, I have two younger brothers. Two *annoying* little brothers. It's pretty much the worst ever.

"Christmas?" This is March; that holiday is long gone.

"Yep, with that green dress and those awful red streaks you put in your hair, you make me want to watch *Rudolph* and hang ornaments on the tree."

"Whatever! You're the ridiculous one, with your purple tie and sweater vest," I say.

"If you say so, Jolly Old Saint Nick."

"I don't look like Christmas," I tell him, but I walk over to the mirror. The girl who stares back at me isn't happy at all. Instead of the cute black dress I gazed at every time we went to the mall, the one I'd planned to buy for our big concert, I have on a junior bridesmaid dress that's about as pretty as a pillowcase. It's made of some stretchy fabric that bunches up around my waist and digs into my armpits. And it's green. Not the cute emerald green or Kelly green that all the celebrities wear these days, but bright elf green. My brothers are right; with the red streaks in my hair, I'm ready to deck the halls and have myself a merry little Christmas.

"I'm suddenly in the mood for milk and cookies," Lucas says, coming up behind me.

"That's it," I announce. "I refuse to wear this!"

I go to my suitcase and pull out my jeans with the rhinestones that I wore on the drive here because right now, no dress is better than wearing this one. I try to reach behind and unzip the offending dress, so I'll at least look the part of the lead singer even if I'm not rocking out with everyone back at school.

"Not a chance," Mom says. The phone is still up against

her ear, so I pray maybe she's talking to my aunt instead of me. "You're not putting that on," she says, crushing all my hopes.

"But why not? The ceremony is over, and we took a million pictures of me in this awful thing. Can't I wear these now?"

"You're wearing the dress your cousin picked out for you. It's your cousin's night, so you'll do what makes her happy."

What about what makes me *happy? It was supposed to be my night*, I want to say, but it's no use trying to convince Mom. I can tell from the glare she gives me that I won't win this argument.

I try a different approach and decide to talk to Dad instead. He's always the easier one to convince, especially when it involves ice cream before dinner or staying up past my bedtime. Dad's a sucker for my sad face, and sticking out my bottom lip and looking especially pathetic always seals the deal.

I've studied the bus maps, and even though we are almost three hours from home, if I take the six thirty p.m. bus, I might make it back so I can sing with the band. Imagine everyone's surprise and delight if I showed up. They'd be so excited, especially since they were all upset when I broke the news that my parents were making me go to this wedding. It was awful; we all cried a little bit. Well, except Genevieve, who got really, really quiet. She's probably thrilled to be in the spotlight since she only joined a month ago as a backup singer and now she gets to take my spot in the lead.

"Dad, what do you think about taking me to the bus station before you all go to the reception? I can go home early, sing with the band, and stay with Tess."

"Yeah, and he can also drop me off at the airport for a flight to Disney World," Alex says, and I want to scream. "There's no way you're going to be allowed to ride the bus alone."

"Stay out of this," I snap.

"He's right," Dad says. He doesn't even take his eyes off the TV, and I can't believe he's abandoning me instead of being my ally. "That's too dangerous. And besides, you know how excited Mom is for us to spend family time together."

"This is so unfair. It's Heart Grenade's big night. We worked so hard to win the Battle of the Bands at the mall, and now I can't claim our prize."

"We've been over this already, Carmen. You made a commitment to be in your cousin's wedding," Mom says. She's finally hung up the phone, probably so she can direct all her attention toward continuing to ruin my night.

"But that was before we won." I try to reason with her. "When am I ever going to be on TV again?"

"You'll survive," Mom says.

But I'm really not sure I will. Our local station is broadcasting Heart Grenade's concert to everyone during the evening news, and I won't be a part of it.

"You don't understand. Anyone could be watching. I'm pretty sure Taylor Swift got discovered in a similar way."

"And I also bet that she went to all her family weddings," Mom says. She touches up her bright red lipstick in the mirror and doesn't seem to care at all that my life is ending. "It's good to spend time as a family."

"Well, you got your wish," I say.

"How about you try to have fun? You might even find that being at this wedding isn't so awful, *mi pajarita*."

She tries to pull me into a hug that I most definitely do not want.

I wiggle out of it and back away. "Fun? You don't understand anything! When I have daughters, I'm always going to listen to them and make sure I support everything they want to do."

I huff and puff all the way to the bathroom to make sure everyone knows how mad I am. I slam the door and sit on the edge of the bathtub.

This is a million times more horrible than I'd imagined. I pull out my cell phone and send a text to Tess.

Help! Emergency! Come save me STAT!!! This is a tragedy! I need to be with all of you!

I wait for her to reply and wish that she really could come to save me. But when you're stuck an entire state away in a hotel room, that's pretty much impossible.

Someone bangs on the door.

"Time's up, Mrs. Claus. I need to get in there," Alex yells.

I turn on the water in the tub full blast to drown him out, scroll through my Instagram feed, and torture myself with picture after picture of everyone getting ready for the dance. I burst out laughing at a picture from earlier in the afternoon of my classmate (and Tess's mortal enemy) Mariah with a green face mask on and the caption, *Do you all like my makeup for the dance? Perfect, right?!* I scroll through and pause on a cartoon one of my classmates drew of Heart Grenade's logo. *Can't wait to hear my favorite band live* is written on the bottom.

"My life is over!" I wail.

"Carmen, open up right now! This isn't funny," Lucas whines. "I drank two cans of soda and need to use the bathroom."

"Should've thought about that before you made fun of my dress."

I hear Dad yell something with my name in it, so I know it's only a matter of time before he comes over and tells me to open the door.

I grab for my phone as it lights up, telling me I have a text.

Except it isn't from Tess.

It's from Genevieve.

THE Genevieve, who is taking my place tonight as lead singer.

A.k.a. . . . the last person in the world I want to hear from.

Hope the wedding is fun. Wish you were here!

I feel a little better. At least the band is thinking of me.

I'm about to respond when another message from her pops up on the screen.

Any last-minute advice?

Seriously? She's asking me for advice? That's like kicking someone when they're down.

I don't want to give her advice; I want to be up there onstage. I fight back tears while Lucas continues to pound on the door and Alex sings Christmas carols. And his song choice couldn't be better, because it's going to be a "Silent Night" for me as the lead singer of Heart Grenade.

GENEVIEVE { 6:31 P.M. }

IT'S MY FIRST NIGHT AS THE LEAD SINGER OF Heart Grenade. And if I have anything to say about it, it'll also be my last.

I've always loved to sing. I still love to sing. The thing is, I only love to *perform* if I'm in the background or part of a group, where my voice can blend with everyone else's. When I sing at church or in select choir at school, it's impossible to pick individual voices apart, so I'm able to squash down the panic that tries to claw its way up from my stomach every time I step onto a stage. But just the thought of being pinned alone in a bright white spotlight like a spider trapped under a plastic cup is enough to make me feel sick.

Why does Carmen's cousin have to get married *today* of all days? And what was I *thinking* when I told the band I'd fill in as lead singer? I should've told them I wasn't ready for this. But none of the Heart Grenade girls know me very well yet—I only joined the band last month, after they kicked out their last backup singer for skipping too many rehearsals—and I was afraid they'd drop me, too, if I said no. Then again, they'll probably throw me out anyway if I mess up tonight for them.

I figure maybe I'll feel more confident if I at least look like the lead singer I'm supposed to be, so I change into the outfit my best friend, Sydney, helped me pick out. Shimmery silver tank top. Leopard-print skirt with tulle underneath, a hand-me-down from my cousin. Lime green jacket. Glittery black tights. I top it all off with my lucky green Chuck Taylor high-tops.

I am a rock star, I think to myself. But when I look in the mirror, I can't totally tell whether this look says *rock star* or *victim of a fabric store explosion*. Syd will be able to help when she gets here. She's really into fashion blogs all of a sudden.

There's a knock on my bedroom door. "Gen?" Papa calls. "You dressed?"

"Yeah." My dads come in, and I spin around to show off my outfit. "Too much?"

"Definitely not. You look great," Dad says. Then again, I'm not positive he's the best judge. His shirt is such a vivid shade of orange that it almost hurts to look at it, and he's not even dressed up for a special occasion. All he's doing tonight is watching TV with Papa.

A little shiver of fear zings up my spine when I remember that one of the things they'll be watching is *me*. They wanted to come to school and see my performance live, but I told them it would be much cooler to see me on TV. Really, it's mostly because I don't want to see their faces fall if I completely freeze up.

"Want me to do a zigzag braid for you?" Papa asks, and I nod. He's amazingly good with hair for someone who shaves his head. Sydney always tries to do cool stuff with my mass of wild curls, but she can never wrestle them into submission the way Papa can. Syd's hair is the complete opposite of mine: blond and soft and stick straight.

I sit down on the floor, and Papa perches behind me on the bed and starts braiding. The movement of his fingers against my head is soothing. "How're you feeling about tonight?" he asks.

I've never told Dad and Papa how scared performing

makes me—I don't want them to know I'm not brave like they are. They're in this amazing gay men's chorus, and both of them sing lead all the time. Neither of them has any idea I was offered a solo in this spring's choir concert and turned it down because I was terrified. They think I auditioned for Heart Grenade because I wanted to try singing a different kind of music, not because I thought it might help me get comfortable singing in smaller groups.

So I try to shove all my panic to the very bottom of my stomach before I shrug and say, "I feel okay, I guess."

Dad must hear the tiny shake in my voice, because he reaches over and rubs my shoulder. "You're going to be wonderful. I'm so excited for you."

"Carmen did a great job at the Battle of the Bands, but I think you have a better voice," Papa says. "I heard you practicing in the shower yesterday, and you sounded spectacular."

I know he's trying to boost my confidence, and I love him for it. But the thing is, it doesn't really matter which of us sounds better. Carmen can handle the pressure of being a lead singer, and I can't.

"Thanks," I say anyway. I'm glad I'm facing away from him so I don't have to force a smile.